D1491914

# GIVE A DOG
# A NAME

**Portway Large Print**

**Published by us~
chosen by you**

# GIVE A DOG
# A NAME

# GERALD HAMMOND

## A Portway Large Print Book

PUBLISHED BY
Remploy Press, Halifax

First published in 1992
by
Macmillan London Limited

© Gerald Hammond 1992

Published in large print 1994
by arrangement with
Macmillan London Limited

*The right of Gerald Hammond to be identified as the
author of this work has been asserted by him in accordance
with the Copyright, Designs and Patents Act 1988*

ISBN 0 7066 1036 9

This Large Print Edition is published
by Remploy Ltd in association
with Library Services Ltd, a
Library Association Company.

Typeset and Printed by
Page Bros, Norwich
Bound by Remploy Ltd
Halifax

# ONE

I was along as the driver of the battered old estate car and so had stayed carefully just on the right side of the breathalyser but, when we got back to Three Oaks, Isobel, one of my partners, was undeniably tipsy. Only Lucy was truly sober. Nobody had offered her a drink of anything more stimulating than water although her efforts had been the cause of Isobel's celebration.

Lucy was a black and white springer bitch of our own breeding. We had intended to keep her as a brood bitch, but an early case of pyometra had necessitated a hysterectomy and put an end to that plan. The alternative was to sell her as a trained gun dog; but she had responded so well in advanced training that we had decided to run her in a trial or two. A spayed bitch might not be everyone's choice as a shooting companion, but a spaniel that was not only trained but had shown a few successes in field trials would have substantially enhanced value in the market-place.

In age, Isobel was the senior partner by some years. Anyone judging by appearance alone would have guessed her to be a fountain of good works and fancy knitwear, destined to become a formidable old lady. But Isobel had started life as a vet and had remained in touch with gun dogs during her long marriage. She had proven to be a winning handler. She might be short of the patience needed for training dog after dog, varying the regime to suit the personality of each pupil; but that was my forte. Instead, she had the ability to stay calm under the stress of competition conditions. When the bird was a runner, the spaniel getting out of control and the nearest judge beginning to look suspicious, Isobel would be thinking her way through circumstances which would reduce many handlers, myself included, to a state of impotent whistling. She also had the gift of robust good health which I lacked. Thanks to Isobel's firmness and her apparently intuitive knowledge of which way a pricked pheasant was going to run, Lucy had won an open stake at only her second attempt.

There had been fog on the Cairn o' Mount and a tailback at the Tay Road Bridge. It was late when my headlamps swept across the face of the converted farmhouse and woke the dogs in their wired-in kennels. They knew the sound of the car, but any excuse to bark was a break in the monotony of the long night. I noticed an unfamiliar car, unostentatiously expensive, tucked against the end of the barn.

The outside lamp came on and then more light fanned out as Beth, my wife and the third partner in the kennels, came out. Even in the harsh light of the headlamps she looked like a teenager. She was at my window as I brought the car to a halt. 'There's somebody waiting,' she said.

This had to be urgent or she would first have asked how we had fared and whether Lucy was undamaged by barbed wire and stray pellets. 'I'll come right away,' I said.

Beth stooped to speak past me. 'It's Isobel he wants to see.'

'You and Isobel should be putting Lucy away,' I said firmly. Isobel was not going to meet any clients that evening. 'Lucy's been dried. She's had her meal and we let her out for a pee when we filled the car up at Stracathro.'

Beth looked at Isobel and nodded quickly. She was no stranger to Isobel's habit of going on the toot whenever there was an excuse for a celebration. 'Stardust refused again,' she said.

I sighed. The statement would have sounded mad to a stranger but I knew exactly what Beth meant. Stardust was another of our breeding prospects, but during her previous season, rather than accept the service of either of the chosen studs she had not only refused to stand but had made spirited attempts to castrate each of them. Her seasons were slightly irregular but she had seemed to be arriving at the most propitious time.

The drizzle which had plagued us all day in Aberdeenshire had given way to frost in Fife. Ice had been jangling under the wheels for the last

3

few miles. 'Take my coat,' I said, 'or you'll freeze.'

I gave Beth my coat and bolted into the house before the cold could seep right through me. I was met by warmth and the smell of cooking. Isobel and I had stopped for a snack with our drinks at Fettercairn, but Beth always goes on the assumption that I have eaten nothing since leaving home.

In our old-fashioned sitting-room, a cheerful fire was burning. A cup of tea, still full, had cooled beside one of the wing-chairs but the visitor was on his feet. As with his car, his clothes managed to be both expensive and at the same time modest. He was in his forties although premature baldness made him look older, but his movements were brisk and animated. I put him down as a businessman, usually very calm and assured but for the moment very much off-balance. I get these moments of insight from time to time and sometimes they turn out to be correct.

He came straight to the point, speaking in staccato bursts with an accent that was either English or from one of the top Scottish schools.

'Lansdyke,' he said. 'Arthur Lansdyke. I live at Kilcolm, just this side of Cupar. Thank God you've turned up at last! Hope you can help me out.'

'We will if we can,' I said.

'Thanks. You certainly can.' He looked at his

watch. 'I've got about ten minutes, then I'll have to go or I'll miss my plane. All hell's broken loose on a contract in Switzerland. I've got to be there by morning and God knows when I'll be able to get home – could be a day or a fortnight. My dog, Horace, went AWOL during the morning. He does that sometimes, he's an occasional wanderer, and I took my eye off him for a few seconds. Around four, just when I was ready to leave, he dragged himself home with shot in him. I have an arrangement with a local kennels, but they didn't want the responsibility of taking him to the vet and when I managed to reach my usual vet he was unhelpful; he'd treat the dog but he wouldn't keep him overnight and deliver him to the kennels when he'd finished doing whatever was necessary. He gave him a pain-killer and the poor old chap's comatose at the moment, but that's as far as the vet was prepared to go before tomorrow.

'Then I remembered that you have kennels and one of the partners is a vet, am I right?'

'Quite true,' I said.

'So I came straight here. Could you do whatever's needed and then keep him until I get back? Carte-blanche.'

I thought about it. His genuine concern over his dog was very much in his favour. 'We don't usually board,' I said, 'but we're not expecting our usual quota of litters so I suppose we could find room. What sort of dog, and how bad is it?'

'Springer. Great gun dog and a pedigree as long as a punt-gun. I . . . I don't know how bad it is. I heard him wailing – a sound like nothing I've heard before, it sent shivers up my back! When I went out to him, his wounds were weeping.'

'Anything other than blood?'

'Not that I could see. He was having difficulty dragging himself along.' Mr Lansdyke passed a shaking hand across a face which looked grey. 'I don't know what the hell can have happened. He never chases sheep.'

I made a noncommittal noise. Every owner says the same. Some even invent elaborate lies to hide the fact that they peppered the dog themselves in a moment of carelessness.

He sensed my doubt. 'It's true,' he said. 'I had him trained that way and I've kept it up. He thinks sheep are all in the mind. He's a randy bugger, though. Probably went after somebody's bitch. But shooting would seem a bit drastic even in defence of a favourite daughter.' He looked at his watch again. 'Got to go in a minute.'

'Inoculation certificates?' I asked. His hurried style of speech was infectious.

'Here. He's had all his shots.' Mr Lansdyke pulled out a wad of papers and picked out a vet's record card from between his passport and an airway ticket folder. He followed it with several bank-notes. 'And a deposit. All right?'

'I suppose. Where's the dog now?'

'Your kennel-maid carried him through to the surgery.'

'My partner will be here shortly and she'll see to him. You know, you could have left him with Beth and gone for your plane.'

He nodded while shrugging his way into a good sheepskin coat. 'Seemed a bit young to be left in charge of a wounded dog.'

Beth's absurdly juvenile appearance often gives rise to that misapprehension. 'She's nearly thirty,' I said. But he was already on his way out to his car.

At the back of the house a small outbuilding had been tiled and converted into a miniature surgery. The intention had been to make a place where Isobel could attend to the needs of our dogs in conditions of relative sterility; but the nearest vet, who wanted to retire but did not have the heart to turn away a sick animal, had adopted a rude and unsympathetic manner which was causing many of his former clients to turn to Isobel in emergencies. As a result, the surgery had expanded in equipment and facilities while the cost had been offset by the fees that she brought in.

The patient, Horace, was indeed comatose. I found him lying flat out on the stainless steel operating table which took up about half the floorspace in the tiny room. Beth had left a bowl of water within his reach but he was snoring gently, untroubled by the dozen or more pellet-holes, some of which were still oozing a little blood. None looked dangerous to my inexpert eye, but one or two were perilously near to joints and it was quite possible that stomach contents were leaking into the body cavity. The pattern of punctures was uneven, but I guessed that the dog had been fired at from not less than thirty yards or else that the shot had been scattered by intervening leaves. In either eventuality, most of the pellets should not have penetrated too deeply. A spaniel's thick pelt, especially the thicker coat of winter, is at least a partial protection against shot.

My partners joined me soon after Mr Lansdyke's car was out of sight. Beth had told Isobel what little she knew and I filled in the details.

Isobel squinted at the patient. 'Hot water,' she said.

'We have a new steriliser,' Beth reminded her.

'Not for the instruments. Black coffee,' Isobel said. 'And I'd better eat something. Another half-hour won't hurt him.'

'Come along,' Beth said. She led the older woman through to the cluttered, shining kitchen, the heart of the house, and settled her in one of the basket chairs in front of the range. I followed and took the other chair. Beth loaded two soup-plates with a meat and vegetable stew which we took on our knees. My fickle appetite was returning and I managed to pick away at the stew, but Isobel ate with dedication.

Beth put mugs of coffee beside us. 'Do you want me to sterilise some forceps and shave around the pellet-wounds?' she asked.

'Forceps, yes. The smallest we've got. Don't shave him yet,' Isobel said. 'That only makes it more difficult to pick out any hairs that've been carried into a pellet-wound. And you'd end up stripping the whole dog. If he wakes up naked among strangers, the shock'd be worse than being shot.'

'Some of the shot may have gone deep,' I said.

'Probing often does more damage than leaving a pellet or two under the skin. We'll have to pick out as much as is easily reached and give him a powerful antibiotic. Somebody phone Henry and tell him to come for me in about an hour.' Henry was her husband.

I reached for the kitchen extension.

'If Henry's also had a few,' Beth said, 'tell him to stay where he is. I'll run Isobel home. I'll go and get everything ready in the surgery.'

Henry, when he answered the phone, seemed quite sober. I explained that we had a minor emergency and he promised to come over as soon as he had had something to eat.

'Eat but don't drink,' I said. Henry, although well on in years, was another who liked his drink on occasions. Sometimes I looked on him as a substitute father; at others, when the drink had been flowing, I treated him more as a slightly retarded son.

Isobel finished her stew and drank her coffee. She studied her fingers at arms' length, more, I think, to test her eyesight than the steadiness of her hands. 'Ready now,' she said. 'You can come and hold his head, John. I don't want to give him any more dope if I don't have to.'

Peppered dogs were not uncommon during the shooting season. Beth had prepared Horace meticulously. Knowing Isobel's methods of old, she was ready with a bottle of gentian violet to dab each wound as soon as the pellet was out not for purposes of asepsis but as a marker, to avoid damage by further probing in a puncture from which the pellet had already been extracted. The surgery was very cramped with three of us in it, or four if you counted Horace. Isobel worked with calm professionalism. It seemed that food, coffee and responsibility were all that was needed to restore her to sobriety.

Horace roused as Isobel began work. Sedated though he was, he could feel the pain; but he seemed to take comfort from my touch and a few kind words. He was a good little dog and accustomed to giving his trust to humans.

He suffered patiently until Isobel straightened up and dropped the forceps into the steriliser. 'That's all I can do for now,' she said. 'He'll have to be watched. I think he'll make a full recovery

10

but it may take time. Some of the tendons are bruised. I just hope there's no nerve damage.'

I left them applying tiny sterile dressings to the few shaved areas where wounds were still weeping and went through to the sitting room. Henry had arrived and was sitting patiently in front of the fire. As usual, he looked old and exhausted but this was illusory. Henry might look his age, but the years sat easily on his physique. He was, as always, fully alert and could probably have walked me off my feet.

'How's the patient?' he asked.

'Isobel seems satisfied. She'll be through in a minute or two. You'll have a beer? Or have you . . . ?'

'No I haven't,' he said indignantly, as though I had accused him of some minor perversion. 'I've been out long-netting with Charlie Aimes. Brought you a dozen rabbits for the dogs or for the table, if Beth wants them. Beer would be fine.'

I poured two beers and added a log to the fire.

'A shot dog, you said on the phone. Worrying sheep?'

'The owner said not,' I told him. 'Take that for what it's worth. He probably doesn't know. The dog may have been having a private hunt in the bushes and got in the way of somebody rabbiting.'

'Well, don't look at me,' Henry said. 'We didn't go out until dusk so we didn't take guns.'

We were talking idly around the subject of Lucy's triumph when Isobel joined us a minute or two later. She was carrying a small white enamel bowl. 'Ah, drinks!' she said, as though the idea was a complete novelty. She dropped into a chair. 'Could I have a pink gin?' My slight hesitation must have shown. 'I only drink to keep up my strength,' she added.

I fetched her a pink gin.

Henry looked at her mournfully. 'Is the bowl in case your stomach rebels?' he enquired.

Isobel snorted. 'I'd need a bigger bowl than this, after one of Beth's meals.' She made a long arm and handed Henry the bowl. 'See what you make of this.'

Henry looked into the bowl. 'I'll be damned!' he said. 'I thought for a moment you'd got some rape or turnip seed out of his coat.'

I was too tired and lazy to get out of my chair again. 'What's up?' I asked him.

'Two different sizes of shot. Some bird-shot about number sevens. And half a dozen much bigger. Threes, I think.'

'I thought it was odd,' Isobel said. 'Somebody gave him both barrels.'

Henry took a pull at his beer and then looked down into the enamel bowl again. 'It's not unknown for somebody to load a cartridge with a mixture of shot sizes.'

'If you're thinking of the Remington Duplex

cartridge,' I said, 'it uses two very close sizes of small shot.'

'I was thinking of amateur loaders. Sometimes they try out the theory that a little small shot mixed with the larger gives them a better chance of a head shot at geese. Unsound in theory and it never throws a good pattern, but they will do it.'

'Not this time,' Isobel said. 'The larger pellets would have penetrated deeper than the small ones. Wouldn't they?'

'Much deeper,' Henry said.

'That's what I thought. Well, they didn't. As soon as I noticed the difference I started paying attention. Unless the dog was hit from close by, shot doesn't usually go much deeper than the skin, thank the Lord. That's where the larger pellets were, so I picked most of it out. It was centred around the backside and legs. The smaller shot had caught him from in front and gone deeper. Some of it was inaccessible and I had to leave nine or ten pellets in him. They shouldn't matter. He was lucky. The small shot missed his eyes and the large shot missed his testicles.'

'Somebody caught him hanging round where he'd no business to be,' I said. 'After the chickens, perhaps. They shoved the first two cartridges that came to hand up the spout. Plenty of men carry a few threes with them, in case they get the chance of a goose or a hare. They took one shot at him and fired again as he was getting out of range.'

'Wrong way round,' Henry said. 'The shot in front would have been deeper in than the ones in his bum. Somebody must have chased him off with a shot up the backside and then reloaded with threes, followed him up and ambushed him. Or else there were two of them.'

Beth arrived in time to hear his last few words. 'I've given him a clean bed in the surgery,' she said. 'But, John, whoever would do a thing like that? To a spaniel! I can just imagine somebody firing one shot to chase him off. But to follow him up! I think that's awful!'

'So do we,' Isobel said gently. 'But not everybody has a tender heart like yours. This may come as a shock to you, Beth, but some people don't like dogs very much. Not even spaniels,' she added firmly as Beth opened her mouth to protest.

Beth looked unconvinced.

The following day was one of our quiet Sundays. On one Sunday a month I held what had become known as my Masterclass, to which amateur handlers brought their dogs for help, advice and a chance to chat or to show off their progress.

But this was not a Masterclass day. In theory, it was an idle day at Three Oaks Kennel, by which I mean that the dogs were given a respite from training and there was little for us to do except to deal with any urgent inquiries, clean the runs, exercise the dogs, feed the puppies and inspect the entire stock for wounds, ticks, fleas, mites, infections, unexpected arrivals into season or the imminence of whelping.

When Isobel, surprisingly bright-eyed considering her state on the previous evening, walked over in mid-morning, Beth, who had come to us first as kennel-maid and still undertook her original duties, was hard at work in the kennels and runs. The office, so-called, was small, cold and inhospitable, so I was updating some records on the kitchen table when Isobel looked in.

'How's my patient?' she asked.

I put off answering until I had completed an entry. 'Very sorry for himself,' I said. 'It hasn't put him off his food. He had a good drink and a meal but I had to carry him outside and support him while he emptied himself. Any attempt to move under his own steam makes him yelp.'

'To be expected,' Isobel said. She went off to check on Horace and came back trying not to look worried. 'He's a sensible little chap,' she said. 'He hadn't tried to lick off any of my dressings. But there's a lot of swelling around some of his joints. And close to the spine. I don't like that.'

'Will he be all right?'

'I hope so. I told you, it'll take time. He can stay in the surgery for now, the warmth may help

15

a little. I really ought to get him X-rayed – it's time we had a machine of our own. And a diathermy unit.'

'Put them on your Christmas list,' I told her. 'Santa may bring you one. Henry might be persuaded to oblige with the other. The partnership certainly can't. It looks as though we're going to be short of pups next year. We may have to buy in.'

'Sad but true,' she said, sinking into the chair opposite. 'Do you want a hand?'

We were finishing up when the phone rang. Arthur Lansdyke was calling from Zurich. I handed the phone to Isobel. From the end of the discussion which I could hear (and without understanding more than a quarter of the veterinary terms used) she was offering him comfort which was no more than lukewarm.

'I'm to take him for X-ray,' she told me when the call finished. 'I can get it done in Cupar tomorrow. He's writing to confirm that what Horace needs, Horace gets.'

'Hence the expression, "Lucky dog",' I said.

'I hope he's lucky. If not, he'll stay lame; and a lame spaniel isn't much use to a shooting man. Mr Lansdyke says that Horace is the best dog he's ever had and that he can learn anything short of doing the housework. Does Beth need help with anything?'

'It's all in hand,' I said emphatically. Isobel had been happy for me when I married Beth, but I knew that she had had reservations. A wife might not be as willing as an employee to work through the weekends so that the partners could enjoy a little leisure. We never missed a chance to reassure her.

Isobel looked at me with amusement. She knew that I was exaggerating. 'Well, I must be off,' she said. 'I'm meeting Henry for lunch at the hotel. Do you fancy joining us for a drink?'

'We'll see what Beth wants to do.'

Beth decided to remain at work but urged me to go with Isobel. Unlike most wives, Beth is always hounding me down to the hotel for a pint or two of Guinness – not because of any hoped-for effect on my virility but because I remain seriously underweight from the illness which had terminated my army career.

We walked the half-mile to the village.

The hotel was an old coaching inn, and the large and rambling bar had been created by throwing together several smaller rooms. The result was an eccentric and rather welcoming charm that attracted customers from some miles around. The bar was busy with Sunday lunchtime drinkers.

Henry had not yet shown his face. Isobel took a shandy, her usual thirst-quencher after an evening on the tiles, and settled at a corner table. I was about to join her with my pint when a young man near me at the bar gave me a small nod of recognition. I knew his face but the sports jacket

17

and flannels looked wrong and I have never been good at recognising people when I meet them suddenly and out of context unless they have their dogs with them. After a few moments of mentally placing him behind counters and trying to visualise him with a dog, I identified him as the local constable who had replaced our recently promoted sergeant.

I paused beside him on my way towards Isobel and exchanged a few words about the weather and how he was settling in at the police house. 'Have there been any recent complaints about sheep-worrying around Cupar?' I asked him when the courtesy topics were out of the way.

'No, nothing at all,' he said, before remembering that information should never be given away without a quid pro quo. 'Why do you want to know?'

If there had been no sheep-worrying reported, I could speak freely. 'Somebody brought us in a spaniel with shotgun pellets in him. The owner says that he doesn't know how it happened, but he may be covering up his own carelessness. If a man takes a shot at ground game in thick cover and the dog's hard on its heels, accidents can happen. I was just curious.'

The constable lost interest. The law does not require accidents to be reported which do not entail injury to humans. 'That's probably it,' he said. 'There's been no sheep worrying.'

I joined Isobel and repeated the information.

She shrugged. 'It could have been anything,' she said. 'I saw in the paper that a man was fined for shooting a dog that raided his dustbin. Shot it dead.'

The farmer whose land adjoined ours, Andrew Williamson, was standing at the bar, talking to somebody who had his back to us but frowning at me over the other's shoulder. Williamson and I had got off on the wrong foot when I arrived at Three Oaks and we had stayed on it ever since. I was not alone in his disfavour. General opinion was that he liked nobody, not even his own wife. When he fell out with her, he was inclined to descend on the inn like a busload of football supporters and drink himself into a stupor; but the Williamsons must have been in harmony just then because he was sipping his way slowly through a half-pint.

That conversation ended, apparently in disagreement, and the other man loomed over us and then sat down opposite Isobel. His strong features would have suited a larger man – except that his chin was fractionally too near his nose, giving him a toothless appearance although he was by no means short of teeth. He was Dan Sievewright, another farmer from several miles away and an occasional client.

'Yon Williamson's as daft as they come,' he said without greeting or preamble. 'I was coming to see you. Getting low on dogfood. You'll drop me over the usual order?'

I had no particular liking for Sievewright with his abrupt and rather hectoring manner and I resented being required to deliver an order which he could as easily have collected for himself or bought in Cupar. But I owed him an occasional favour. He allowed me to train dogs on his land, which was well suited to checking the steadiness of a dog to rabbits or giving a youngster its first introduction to pigeon.

'I'll bring it over tomorrow,' I said.

Isobel, who had been brooding, woke up suddenly. 'If you're going that way,' she said, 'you could take Horace in for his X-ray. I'll phone for an appointment.' It seemed that I was everybody's errand-boy.

'What's this?' Sievewright asked. 'Your spaniels having hip-trouble?'

'Nothing of the sort,' Isobel said coldly. She had no more liking for Sievewright than I had and the suggestion that we had been careless enough to breed hip dysplasia into our stock was a deadly insult. 'A client brought us in a dog with some pellets in him. Nobody seems to know how it happened.'

'I could make a guess,' Sievewright said. Farmers seem to have single-track minds where other people's dogs are concerned.

'When I bring your dog-meal over, is it all right if I fetch a dog along for a workout?'

He hesitated and then shook his head. 'Leave

it a week or two,' he said. 'We're planning a family shoot.'

I shrugged. A farmer has every right to say who may shoot over his land and when, but I was surprised. Apart from the rabbits and an occasional visiting flock of pigeon, the farm held only a single small covey of partridges and two or three pheasants which had wandered in from further afield; and as far as I knew his only family was the brother who shared his farm and with whom he was usually at loggerheads. I was going to ask what he expected to put in the bag when he recognised somebody at the other end of the bar and left us with no more farewell than to remind me about his dogfood.

## TWO

One of the few advantages of being self-employed, I sometimes thought, was that Monday mornings were no different from any other morning. My outlook on that particular Monday morning may have been jaundiced by the knowledge that somebody was shooting spaniels in the neighbourhood, but the morning seemed to be all that a Monday morning was supposed to be – dull and dispiriting without even being wet enough to make an excuse for rushing through the work and then stretching out in front of the fire with a good book or a cosy wife. Even the morning mail failed to produce replies to recent letters to the Kennel Club about registrations. I wondered whether London hadn't been bombed out of existence, and the Scottish media either had not yet found out or did not consider the news to be worth reporting. Both hypotheses were perfectly credible.

A large bag of kennel meal and a smaller bag of beef cracknel went onto the back seat of my old estate car. Isobel had left a note for the surgery where she had been a partner before her marriage, detailing the X-rays to be taken. Horace had gratefully accepted a handful of biscuits but I had to carry him out into the garden and then to the car. I wondered whether he was genuinely unable to walk or had merely decided that he preferred to be carried everywhere.

I took a back road towards Cupar. Along the way, I passed the farm that Dan Sievewright shared with his less dour brother, but I drove on. After another mile, I passed the end of a driveway almost hidden between trees. I had passed that way a hundred times before without noticing it particularly, but with Horace and his master fresh in my mind the neat sign 'Kilcolm' caught my eye. That was the address that Arthur Lansdyke had given me. I slowed the car. The roof of a substantial house showed through the trees.

In Cupar, Isobel's one-time partner, now an elderly man but still a competent professional, read her notes and asked after her health and the state of the business while settling Horace under a new-looking X-ray machine. He refused to comment to me on another vet's patient, but he confirmed that he knew of no recent instances of sheep-worrying.

I used my voice and hands to soothe Horace until he relaxed and lay still under the X-ray camera.

As I had expected, the X-rays would not be ready until after midday, which would give me time to have a word with one of the Sievewrights while delivering the dogfood. If somebody was shooting spaniels in the area, I would be easier in my mind if I knew who and why. There had been one or two instances, although not very recent, of malicious dog-poisoning. I settled Horace back on the dog-bed in the rear of the car and drove out of Cupar again.

The farmhouse at Easter Colm stood within a few yards of the road. I parked at the door and while I waited I admired the last of the roses in the farmhouse garden. Several new bushes had been planted. The brothers were both single and it was George who usually attended to the garden. Although neither brother seemed to take any pleasure in the garden and other neighbours had told me that there was never a flower in the house, the garden was always immaculate – in contrast to the farmhouse, which was in a dilapidated state with dark scars of rot showing through the paint of the windows and one or two slates standing up in the guttering.

I had seen Dan tinkering with a tractor between the barns as I arrived, but I was sure that George, his brother, would put in an appearance. Neither brother ever let the other make a move about the place unsupervised. I already had Dan's opinion and I would value another from George.

But it was Dan who emerged, frowning and wiping his hands on a rag, from between the nearer barn and the calf-shed, with his two collies at heel. I got out of the car to meet him. The dogs sniffed suspiciously at my legs and then decided to ignore me.

'You've brought the dogfood,' Dan said.

'I wasn't going to take you away from your tractor. I thought George might come out.'

'George is away,' he said.

'Really?' I said. This was unheard of. George was the home-lover, rarely leaving the farm except, rumour had it, to make assaults on the virtue of any girl or lady for miles around who happened to have caught his fancy.

'Yes, really.' Dan tried, unsuccessfully, to mimic my accent, which army life had Anglicised. Then he decided to be more communicative than usual. 'There's a farm for sale over in the west. This place isn't big enough for both of us.'

His last sentence might be true, but in the

circumstances it also had a taste of a bad Western film. Farm management should never be by two equal partners unless their responsibilities are clear-cut and separate. Otherwise, every decision becomes subject to endless argument.

'You must have been doing better than most, if you can afford to expand,' I said.

He grunted. 'There's ways. Sale and lease-back. If he decides to take it on, I'll not be needing as much meal from now on.'

'The house will seem empty.'

'I like it that way.'

I gave him the bags of dogfood and he paid for it without offering a word of thanks for the free delivery.

'Do you get many wandering dogs around here?' I asked him.

'A few.'

'How about Arthur Lansdyke's spaniel?'

'That bogger!' He glanced at my car, where Horace was rolled into a tight liver-and-white ball. 'Is Horace the yin as got himself shot? Can't say I'm surprised. A dog's either a wanderer or it's not. Aye raking about, is that one. How's he doing?'

'He may not do any more raking about for a long time, if ever. We don't know yet.'

'That'll make a change. Mr Lansdyke's away a lot, at the Glenrothes factory or away round the world. As for that wife of his . . .'

'He's married?' I wondered why I had supposed that Mr Lansdyke was single and then realised that I had assumed it because a man with a wife at home had no need to book his dog into kennels.

'Oh aye.' Sievewright seemed amused. 'He's married. That's for sure. But she can't abide dogs and especially that yin. Often, he'll take the dog into Glenrothes with him, but if he's tentless enough to leave the dog at home when he goes abroad it's my belief she lets it out a-purpose, hoping it'll get itself run over or caught chasing the lambs.'

That explained why Horace had been booked into kennels. 'When the dog's on the loose,' I said, 'where does he usually make for?'

'Comes past here, sometimes, looking for food. Ignored the sheep so far, I'll say that much for him.'

'Was he here on Saturday?'

'Not that I noticed. He may well've passed by on his way to Mr Ellingworth's place. That fat, glaikit cocker spaniel of his is on heat again. You can shoot over the farm if you want,' he added. 'Wi' George away we've had to cancel the shoot.'

'Thanks,' I said. 'I'll come back within the next few days. I'll let you get on with your tractor now.'

'You're not doing me any favours,' he said gloomily. 'It's taken them ten days to get the part and now I'm boggered if it'll fit. Ah well, can't stand here havering all day.' He turned away without another word and carried the bags into the house.

My watch told me that the X-rays would not be ready yet. I decided to pay a call on Tony Ellingworth who lived, with his wife and a multitude of young daughters, another half-mile back along the road towards home in what had once been the small manse to a since-demolished church but was now the hub of a smallholding. From Easter Colm I could see the trees that marked his boundary.

I had met Ellingworth on several occasions. Once, he had burst through the hedge while I had been giving a spaniel some training on the rabbits which infested the set-aside land just beyond his boundary to upbraid me for my cruelty in shooting the rabbits – this despite the fact that the same rabbits regularly decimated his vegetables and that he had no objection to eating the lambs obtained from the few sheep he managed to graze, provided that somebody else did the butchering for him. Another time, he came to Three Oaks to scrounge free advice about the health of his spaniel.

I had no personal quarrel with Ellingworth although he represented a type of hypocrite which I particularly disliked. He seemed to me to live in a dream-world of self-deception. He was a leftover of the waning fad for self-suffi- ciency, but his efforts at raising produce for con- sumption by his family were so disorganised that

I could only assume that he had private means. He had come from some city to live in his own vision of the countryside, without making the least effort to understand country ways or the reasons for them, just as he was a bird-watcher without any understanding of ecology or the effects of climate and predation on food-chains. In short, any study that he had made of the wildlife he professed to love had been made in the school of Walt Disney and his loud support for every 'green' issue was no more than lip-service.

He was the last person I would have expected to shoot a spaniel or even to tolerate the presence of a shotgun, but when I turned the car between the high hedges of honeysuckle and rambling roses that surrounded the Old Manse – hedges which were a picture when in flower but looked unkempt in early winter – there he was on the gravel with a cheap over-under trap-gun in his hands, looking nervous but determined. In my astonishment I nearly forgot to brake. I pulled up short of him with no more than a slight slither on the gravel but he made an exaggerated leap to the side and jerked the gun in a threatening and dangerous movement that would have got him sent home in disgrace from almost any well-run shoot.

A bonfire of good compostable materials was blazing merrily just where I would expect it to do most damage to the overhead limbs of a fine beech.

Ellingworth was a tall man and almost as thin as I was. His nose was narrow and pocked with enlarged pores. A straggly beard failed to conceal pouting lips, a weak chin and an Adam's apple that bobbed around like a boxer on the ropes.

Even allowing for the older children being at school, the place seemed quiet. There was no sign of Mrs Ellingworth, who usually appeared to greet visitors. She was a quiet woman, very feminine and with the smile of a happy angel when she had cause to produce it. As I got out of the car, the fat cocker bounced towards me with a greeting and circled round me. I could see no puffiness in her hinder parts, so her season was over.

Ellingworth approached, bristling. He was not one to pass up a chance to make a justifiable complaint about my driving. I decided to strike first. 'Either shoot me,' I said, 'or point that thing somewhere else. You don't have to protect the virtue of your daughters from me.' One of his few virtues, in my eyes, was that he was very protective of his family. To him, every man was a potential molester.

He had the grace to drop his barrels. 'What the hell do you want?' he asked.

The cocker spaniel was standing up with its paws on my knee – a habit which I would usually have discouraged, but on this occasion it seemed politic to demonstrate that I could count on at least one welcome. I bent and pulled her ears while I replied. 'Somebody put some shot into Mr Lansdyke's springer a couple of days ago,' I said. 'For my own reasons, I'd like to know who. I thought I was wasting my time coming here. You left me in no doubt that you disapproved of shooting.'

'I do, in general,' he said. 'At least of animate targets.'

'Then how come all the armament?'

He glanced down at the gun, made a small movement as if he would have liked to hide it and then combined a sigh and a shrug. 'Sometimes you have to compromise,' he said defensively. 'A fox has been taking my chickens.'

I was hardly surprised. Beyond the house, I could see his chickens in an enclosure surrounded by a wire that a fox could have cleared with ease.

'You needn't expect a fox to come in the middle of the day while you're moving about the place,' I said. 'You'll have to sit up for him.'

'I did,' he said. 'Got one shot at him but I think I missed.' He pointed to a gap in the hedge. Beyond I noticed a line of dark furrows where the Sievewrights had made a start to ploughing their set-aside land. 'And when there's one there's more. The gun's only a borrow and it'll have to go back by this afternoon. The man who lent it to me is fussy about the law.'

The legal period during which a shotgun could be borrowed without variation of either party's shotgun certificate, I seemed to recall, was seventy-two hours. So Ellingworth held a new-style shotgun certificate and the gun had been in his possession before Mr Lansdyke's dog had been peppered. 'You're sure that it was a fox?' I asked him.

'I can tell a fox from a spaniel even if you can't,' he said indignantly.

'Even in the dark?'

'It wasn't as dark as that. There was a moon. Anyway, it couldn't have been Horace; this only happened last night.'

I did not believe him. The previous night had been heavily overcast. 'What size of shot are you using?' I asked.

'I didn't think to look. I've only shot at clay pigeons before now, and then I used whatever they gave me.' He produced an empty cartridge from his coat pocket, glanced at it and then held it up. The letters BB were printed on it.

'And that's the only shot you've fired?'

'Yes.' He suddenly remembered not to be defensive. 'I don't have to answer your questions,' he said.

'What questions?' I asked, turning back to the car.

I left him gobbling indignantly, trying to think of a retort that did not entail answering another

31

of my questions. He was very easy to take a rise out of.

Pulling out of the Ellingworth's driveway, I looked at the dashboard clock. The vet's part-time technician would be coming on duty but I still had time in hand. There was another road to Cupar, an even smaller backroad which followed the other boundary of the Easter Colm land. I decided to return to Cupar by that route. I had only passed that way once or twice but I remem-bered a house by the roadside, a house that I had also half-noticed in the distance during my training walks. And there might be foresters or other workmen who had seen or heard some-thing.

The other road was narrow. It rose, twisted, fell to cross a hump-backed bridge, then climbed and emerged from a pine-wood to skirt the Sieve-wright's stubbles. I slowed to let a hen pheasant get clear. A host of pigeon took fright at the sudden appearance of the car and rose, whirled for a moment and then streamed off towards a safe roost in the woods.

The house was where I remembered it, set on a treeless rise among the fields. It was a neat, square, modern bungalow built of artificial stone and with a brightly tiled roof. It would have looked at home on the edge of a small town, but here it was out of keeping. The garden was precise and tidy – another good display in summer no doubt, but this time the disappointment was in the sterility, with the flowers gone and the earth bare, as against the unkemptness of Ellingworth's hedge. The whole place shouted out the owners' pride and I would not have lived there if I had had it as a gift. But it had a view over most of the Easter Colm land.

I parked and got out of the car. A drizzle had started while I was arguing with Ellingworth and the air, which had felt warm and almost friendly on the more sheltered ground, was carrying it across the crest on a chilly wind so that it was twice as wetting and three times as cold. I hurried up the concrete path to the front door. Somebody was watching me from the picture window but it seemed politer to avoid eye-contact.

The woman who came to answer the chimes was middle aged, and, at first, suspicious of the stranger on her doorstep. I explained that I was trying to find out what had befallen a dog two days earlier and her face cleared.

'I was busy about the house on Saturday,' she said. The mention of the house was enough to bring a thrill of pride into a voice that fell somewhere in the middle range of Scottish voices, neither as broad as a farmer's nor as BBC as the professional class. 'And my husband was away at the football. I took the bairns a walk but we went into the wood. We didn't see any dogs. My dad was in the front garden, the day being fine. Would you like to speak to him?'

I stepped over the threshold. Somewhere at the back I could hear the voice of a child. I guessed the woman's age at fifty and thought that it was probably a grandchild. 'Saturday was a pig of a day in Aberdeenshire,' I said.

'It was nice here. Not very warm, but dry and sunny.' She opened the door to the front room. 'Dad, this gentleman's trying to find out something about a dog. Can you help him?'

The elderly man in the armchair by the window smiled. 'I will if I can,' he said. His accent was slightly broader than that of his daughter. 'Come and sit down.'

I joined him at the window. A walking frame stood between the two chairs. The woman offered us tea or coffee or beer and removed herself in a mild huff when we both refused.

'Tell me the problem,' he said.

'Mr Lansdyke at Kilcolm – you know him?' I broke off to ask.

'We've never met, but Kilcolm . . . that's over there?' His hand, gnarled by arthritis, shook slightly as he pointed towards the fold in the ground that hid Arthur Lansdyke's house. Looking at him, I decided that he must have been an upstanding figure of a man before the years and arthritis took their toll. His face was subsiding, as old faces often do, but there was still a quiet dignity in the bones beneath.

'That's right,' I said. 'His spaniel went for a wander on Saturday and came home with two different sizes of shot in him. He brought the dog to me. I breed and train spaniels not far from here and I'd be happier in my mind if I knew that this was an isolated incident. Also, I'm curious.'

He nodded gravely. 'I can see how you might be worried. Sometimes a gun dog can follow a line too far and lose touch. That's when they're at risk. But how can I help?'

'I wondered whether you'd seen a spaniel or heard shots on Saturday afternoon.'

'Both,' he said.

'Oh? Tell me.' For a moment, I thought that I was nearing the end of my quest.

He chuckled, although it was only a whisper in his throat as though he had almost forgotten how to laugh. 'Not the spaniel you're interested in. Nella – my daughter – helped me out into the garden. I like to feel the sun when I can. I was looking over the farmland. Not much else to do, these days. But my eyes still work, a damn sight better than the rest of me, and I have a good pair of binoculars. You see the small trees where the hedges meet up against the grassy bank?'

When I picked it out, I realised that it was a place I knew well on the ground. A rabbit could often be shot on the banking where a dog was unsighted, giving a young dog its first chance of an easy blind retrieve of something more inter-esting than a dummy. 'I see it,' I said.

'A man was shooting pigeon and he had a spaniel with him. He started with a hide between those trees. I could tell what was going on. Used to shoot woodies myself before my legs gave out on me.' His voice was becoming stronger as he remembered the joy of days now gone. 'He'd placed himself under a flight-line and he was trying to draw them with decoys. Didn't do any good, though. His presence shifted the flight-line and it never returned. I could see them dropping in this side of the crest, but that was out of his sight. If he'd moved, he could have been in among them. As it was, he got about three birds from mid-morning until he gave up a little before three in the afternoon. That was for about a dozen shots, I think, but I couldn't be sure. There was one of those gas-bangers popping away in the distance.'

'You could see them fall?' I asked. The place was nearly half a mile away.

'Not to be sure. I'm judging by the number of times I saw the spaniel go for a retrieve.' He made a sound between a sigh and another attempt at a laugh. 'If you find him, tell him to speak to me before he goes out next time. I usually know where they're feeding and which way they'll fly.'

'I'll speak to you myself,' I said. 'I sometimes shoot there.'

'I've seen you. About once a fortnight you come and do some training, first one dog, then another, sometimes a third, usually spaniels. That is you, isn't it?'

I said that it was.

'Come back any time. Come and talk dogs. I used to train and work spaniels. Best days of my life. Hope you catch the bastard who peppered Mr Lansdyke's dog. Is the little chap going to be all right?'

'We hope so.' I got up to go. 'I have to go and pick up his X-rays now. I don't know your name,' I said.

'Charles Buccleugh.'

He said the name without any emphasis but I recognised it immediately. He had bred one of Lucy's ancestors. 'You were one of the great breeders and handlers of the sixties and seventies,' I told him, as though the news would come as a surprise to him.

'Once upon a time,' he said sadly. 'I had to retire a while back. Then I lost my wife and couldn't look after myself. Nella gives me a home now. It's good of her and I'm glad to be in the country still although' – he paused and looked over his shoulder, lowering his voice – 'it's not quite what I'd have chosen for my last years. But,' he said more cheerfully, 'some of the blood-lines I started are still going on.'

'I have a great-granddaughter of your Cetebos Stanley,' I told him. 'A clever little bitch but the line stops there. She had to have a hysterectomy. You've probably seen me working her, where the man was decoying pigeon. I'll bring her to visit you some time.'

I shook his hand gently, so as not to hurt his old bones, and went out to the car. I was glad to escape. The despondency of the old man, once a vigorous power in the gun dog world but now exiled, lost to the old life and waiting to die, was a reminder that the same fate might be awaiting any of us.

There was one other landowner I could have visited, but time was running out. I headed for Cupar.


## THREE

Isobel and Beth had already eaten before I got back to Three Oaks. Beth was playing on the lawn with some of the younger pups – not so much for pleasure, although I knew that these were among her favourite moments of the day, as to begin the process of humanising and teaching the first elements of responding to the human voice and discipline. She kennelled the pups and joined me as Isobel came out of the house.

'You have the X-rays?' Isobel asked.

When I feel less than sunny, I'm inclined to resent the sort of question which assumes that I might have forgotten to perform some elementary task. I bit back the sarcastic answer that came too easily to my tongue and handed her the large envelope. 'He didn't seem to see anything much wrong,' I said.

I opened the back of the car. Somewhere along the way, Horace had wetted the dog-bed. I called him out but he lay in his own mess, shivering. Beth soothed him until he was calmer. She moved him onto the grass in case he still had something in his bladder, took out the dog-bed for washing and then gathered Horace up tenderly in her arms and carried him inside.

Isobel tapped the envelope and sighed. 'We'll see for ourselves. Not that I hope to see much. Dogs are very like people. The fear of pain can be as off-putting as the pain itself. Give him some more time and then, if he's still not responding, invite him out for a jaunt with the gun. It's amazing how the prospect of a little sport helps them to forget their woes. Very like people,' she repeated. I thought that she was probably getting in a dig at me.

She had been doing the month's accounts in the kitchen. She cleared her tidy groups of papers from an end of the table and I sat down with the snack lunch that Beth had left for me in the oven.

Beth came back from the surgery and began to wash her hands at the sink. 'All he wants to do is to lie there and feel sorry for himself.'

Isobel was holding up the X-rays to the window. 'Shock, fear and bruising,' she said. 'That has to account for it. At first glance, I can't see anything more serious. But you can never be sure. Nerves don't always lie exactly where the books say they should.'

39

Beth brought me a mug of tea. 'You were gone a long time. Where else were you?' she asked me.

I gave them a detailed account of my morning.

'You didn't think of visiting Aubrey Stoneham?' Isobel asked.

'I thought of it,' I said. 'I just couldn't bring myself to do it. Anyway, you'll probably see him at the weekend. Catch him in a good mood after he's put out some poor sod's dog for squeaking.' Stoneham owned a tract of land, including several farms, to the south of Easter Colm. He was also a pillar of the gun-dog world and an experienced trial judge. He was the wrong man to dislike but I disliked him intensely.

'I think you should do the puppy trial on Friday,' Isobel said. 'Sunbeam still works better for you than for me. You can stay overnight. I'll mind the shop.'

'All right,' I said. Dogs, like humans, have their preferences and although Sunbeam (registered name Sunbeam Second of Throaks) was a willing young bitch she would sometimes stop dead and look as though she was wondering just who Isobel thought she was to order her about. 'My traipsing around didn't get us very far,' I added.

'It may have done more good than you think,' Beth said. 'You may have reminded somebody that he can't go shooting at spaniels without questions being asked. And Horace has been

40

very clean up to now. He holds on to it until somebody carries him out onto the grass. I'm wondering if it wasn't nerves that made him let go in the car. Perhaps you went past the place where he was shot.'

'More likely he's just a bad passenger,' Isobel said. 'Being shot, taken away from home and then bumped around by a stranger in a strange car would be enough to make me let go, let alone a nervous dog. Could you make a guess who the pigeon-shooter might have been?'

'It could have been almost anybody,' I said tiredly. 'The Sievewrights don't often refuse permission to shoot pigeon or rabbits. Farmers are so vulnerable when somebody takes a spite against them.' I yawned. The long illness which had ended my career in the army had left a residue of weakness and the old exhaustion was creeping over me.

Beth looked at me sharply. Despite my attempts to cover up, she can always tell when I am under the weather. 'I'll find out,' she said. 'You go and have a lie-down.'

It would have done no good to argue. Beth might look like a pretty teenager but she was an adult woman with a will of iron and, if she decided that I needed a rest, a rest I would have whether I wanted it or not. In fact, I wanted it.

So I went to the couch in the sitting-room and dozed for an hour. I woke refreshed and in a fever to go and catch up with my training schedule which, for the moment, seemed to have slipped out of gear.

But Beth was again adamant. She almost dragged me into the big kitchen and forced me into one of the fireside chairs. 'You can sit down for a mug of soup and a sandwich before you go out into the cold. I'll tell you about my phone-calls.'

'It'll be dark soon,' I protested.

'Isobel was out there putting the older dogs through their paces until a shower started. It's going off now and you'll still have an hour of daylight. When it's dark, you can go and teach the novices some basic obedience under the lights in the barn.' She pushed a mug of scalding soup at me. 'I know who the pigeon shooter was.'

'Did Dan Sievewright tell you?'

'He said he didn't know, but I'm not sure that I believe him. So I started phoning round the pigeon fanatics. The peak rate was finished,' she said quickly, 'and none of the calls lasted for more than a few seconds.' Beth knows that I have a phobia about running up big phone-bills. 'Everybody I phoned suggested one or two names and about the fifth name I spoke to turned out to be the right one. Dougal Henshaw,' she finished triumphantly.

'The man we met wild-fowling on the Tay?'

'That's the one. I had to look him up in the phone-book. His address is Kilcolm Cottage.'

42

'What was he doing, at home on a weekday?' I asked. 'Is he one of the great unemployed?'

'He's working offshore, two weeks on and two off. He said that he was shooting pigeon again yesterday, near Dairsie, until the light went. He was the one on Easter Colm on Saturday and he got five birds, not three, so Mr Buccleugh was wrong, because Mr Henshaw left two of them lying until he picked up his decoys. He says he went straight home afterwards and he didn't see another spaniel all day. And there was a bird-scarer banging away within earshot, so he doesn't know whether he heard any shots or not.'

That agreed with what Charles Buccleugh had said. The subject of Dougal Henshaw seemed to be exhausted for the moment. 'Did Isobel say anything about Horace's X-rays?' I asked.

'She said that they didn't tell her anything she didn't already know.'

I had finished my sandwich. My soup had cooled enough to drink. I swallowed it quickly, pulled on my Wellingtons and went out to do some work with Ember in the barn. He had the common but infuriating habit of dropping the dummy just out of reach and although experience rather than training would probably teach him to bring the retrieve right to hand it was not a habit that I wanted to become fixed.

Overnight, a shallow depression marched away towards Scandinavia and for once the next was not hard on its heels. The Tuesday came in clear and bright and cold.

I had promised myself that I would forget about the mystery of Horace's adventures and devote the whole day to the training sessions which accounted for much of our livelihood. And so, of course, I had barely finished breakfast before I heard a car in the drive.

On the off-chance that it might contain a buyer, I hurried outside. Trained dogs are usually sold out by the middle of the shooting season, but one deal had fallen through when the purchaser had been posted abroad. We had several part-trained dogs for sale and young pups were, as always, available or imminent.

But the car at the door was two-tone, blue and white; and a uniformed constable, a stranger, was getting out of it. The faint hope that he might be snatching a few minutes off duty to shop for a puppy died before he had spoken a dozen words.

'Captain Cunningham?'

'Mister will do,' I said. 'And you are?'

He nodded. 'Peel,' he said. He had a ready smile. 'I'm from Cupar. PC Peel the peeler. Now that we've got that out of the way, you may be able to help me. We've had a complaint about cruelty to a dog. Near Kilcolm it is.' There was a trace of Belfast in his accent. 'The SSPCA man says that he's seen nothing like it.'

I could believe that. Alex Hautry of the

44

SSPCA had a way with animals and he would be good some day, but he was a city boy and also very new to the job.

'Not shot, by any chance?' I asked.

'You'd better see for yourself. Mr Hautry suggested that it would give us a start if you could tell us what breed it had been.'

This sounded messy. I could do without looking at long-dead dogs on a busy morning. On the other hand, I had intended to take Sunbeam for some work on the rabbits at Easter Colm. A young dog soon learns the difference between training and real work, and a reminder that discipline still holds in the field is no bad thing shortly before a serious competition. It would be a chance to probe a little further into the matter of sheep-worrying.

'I know where Kilcolm is,' I said, 'but I'll follow you if you'll give me a minute.'

I fetched Sunbeam and put her in the back of the car. She knew what that meant and her tail was going already. When I fetched a bagged shotgun and a belt of cartridges, the constable's eyebrows went up but he made no comment. I followed him to Kilcolm. He pulled up in the mouth of a track which ran through the wedge of trees behind the house and I parked behind him. He watched as I slung the bagged gun over my shoulder and locked up.

'I'll keep this with me,' I said. 'Estate cars don't lend themselves to hiding things like guns

45

from the passing thief.' A small string of traffic following a tractor lent point to the remark.

He nodded. 'I should warn you that it's not a pretty sight,' he said.

'I expect that I've seen worse.'

The smile came again. 'Probably so.'

He led me along the track, leaving Sunbeam yipping in frustration at being left in the car while the gun was taken for a walk. PC Peel was young, quite tall enough for the police minimum height but very thin and wiry.

'Have you had any complaints about sheep-worrying lately?' I asked him as we walked.

'Not that I've heard. There was a complaint two or three weeks ago – a Labrador led into mischief by a collie. But that was down near Kirkcaldy. The owners have been warned.'

'And no reports of dogs coming home with shotgun pellets in them?'

'No.' He was much less curious than our local man.

We turned off and followed a narrow path through dead bracken. I had already guessed what we would find. The tabloids have a shock-horror story about such things every year or two, so the vulpine corpse hanging from the limb of a tree, indecent in its nudity, came as no surprise to me.

'It seems to have been strangled,' the constable said.

'I'd be interested to know who found it,' I said.

Arthur Lansdyke was still abroad and his spaniel in our care, so who was walking in his woods?

'A local woman, gathering fir-cones for the fire. She's in quite a tizzy, very upset that anyone could do such a thing to a dog.'

'You'd better go and set her mind at rest,' I said. 'They didn't. I'll probably be speaking to Mr Lansdyke on the phone within the next day or two. If you really want to follow it up, I can ask him whether anybody has permission to take foxes here.'

He almost gaped at me. 'This is a fox?'

'Yes.'

'I'd never have known. What killed it? I do a bit of shooting myself – just the clay pigeons – so shot was the first thing I looked for.'

'It was snared,' I said. 'Somebody hung it up to skin it for the pelt and then was too lazy to cut it down and bury it, or even stuff it down a rabbit hole. Or else he had no business being here and he heard somebody coming. I'll deal with it if you like. Or do you want it for evidence?'

Peel made a grimace. 'Evidence of what? They'll not thank me if I fetch it in to the station. You deal with it, sir, and I'll be grateful.'

I usually have a spade with me, more for digging the car out of mud or snow than for burying the dead. I walked back with PC Peel to fetch it.

Half an hour later, we were on Easter Colm.

When we reached the trees where the hedges met I remembered to give Charles Buccleugh a wave, but I had no way of knowing whether he had seen it or not.

## FOUR

That weekend at Dalry, Sunbeam was entered for the spaniel puppy stake on the Friday, which was to be followed next day by a retriever stake in which Beth had entered Jason, her personal Labrador. Jason lived with the other dogs in the kennels but Beth's work with him was entirely on her own account. Whenever I suggested that she was competent to represent the firm by handling one of our spaniels in a trial, she turned white and showed all the signs of imminent nervous breakdown, yet she and Jason made a formidable team in retriever events and it would be only a matter of time before awards would come their way.

So Isobel moved into the farmhouse on the Thursday evening, leaving husband Henry to fend for himself – which he usually managed to do in great comfort. Beth could sense that I was tired, so she drove my big estate car through to Dalry while I dozed beside her and the two dogs curled up together in the back, raising their heads only when the car slowed and showed signs of coming to a halt.

The dogs, as usual, had their beds in the car but we slept that night in a plushy but cold bedroom in a big hotel and went to the novice stake in good time – for my part with the usual butterflies in the stomach.

Isobel might have a better temperament for competition handling than I have but it was true, as she had said, that Sunbeam worked better for me. Even so, Isobel would probably have fared better than I did.

Second time 'down', Sunbeam put up a cock pheasant from the edge of a turnip field. The nearer gun missed it clean and the other shot hastily. The bird spiralled down, a strong runner, and legged it into a large area of reeds. The judge nodded to me and I sent Sunbeam for it. She headed confidently into the reeds. Too soon, I decided that she was off the line and I gave her the stop whistle. She rose on her hind legs to see me over the reeds and I gave her a signal to push her over towards where I thought the bird would be heading. She failed on the retrieve and had her eye wiped. Beth, who was back with the spectators but was watching from a higher viewpoint, said afterwards that Sunbeam was on the line of the runner and given half a minute more would have collected it.

We were unplaced.

On the next day, I was again nervous, at least as nervous as Beth and probably more so. She handled Jason with apparent calm and Jason responded with a performance which, as far as I could see from among the spectators, was faultless. At one point the two judges, one of whom I saw was Aubrey Stoneham, came together to examine one of Jason's retrieves. Surely, I thought, he was not going to be put out for biting down on the retrieve? Not Jason, who had one of the softest mouths I had ever encountered? Often, in the spring, he would bring one of us, quite unharmed, a newly hatched songbird chick which had fallen out of its nest. Replaced in the nest, it would usually thrive.

There was an argument between the judges and one or two glances seemed to be aimed not at Beth but in my direction. Then they came to a decision and the line moved on. Evidently, all was well.

When the trial finished, I was sure that Beth and Jason had to have won. Every other dog had shown some fault, however slight, while Jason had had some of the most difficult retrieves and had never missed a trick. But no trial is over until the judges have given their verdict.

There was a long wait in a draughty farmyard while the judges argued again. At last, they pronounced. Beth and Jason were placed third. First place went to a dog that had several times shown signs of impatience and had only been checked from running-in by a quick word from the handler.

Beth was elated by her placing, her best yet;

but I knew that her dream was to make Jason up to champion status, and only a win would have counted towards that goal. Luck of the draw, I told myself. Judges can make mistakes but they as often err in one's favour as the other way.

We went back to the hotel, fed the dogs and bedded them in the back of the car and then settled ourselves at a small table in the corner of the bar while we waited for dinner to be served. Beth insisted on buying me a pint out of her modest prize money. The room filled with competitors and followers, celebrating or consoling, and began to empty again as those within reach of home trickled away.

Out of the corner of my eye I had been aware of a figure moving closer as the throng eddied. Suddenly a voice said, 'Mind if I join you?' in a tone suggesting that any objection would be irrelevant if not downright impossible.

I looked up. The tall figure of Aubrey Stoneham was looming over us.

If Stoneham had ever been one of my favourite people, this was not the day; but common courtesy required that I get up and pull over a chair for him.

He sat down with a grunt. 'Hard on the feet, a day's judging,' he said. 'Sometimes I think that the Americans have the right idea. I was at a trial over there where the judges were on horseback. Saves their poor old legs and they get a better view from higher up. Viewpoints can be very important.' He paused and looked at me. He had a highly coloured face with a slightly twisted mouth. He also had a habit of looking at me, down a proud nose, as though I had been a dog which had just peed on its retrieve. There seemed to be a colder than usual gleam in his eye. 'Hard luck on your wife, I thought. For a while, she seemed to have it in the bag.'

I make it a rule never to argue with a judge. He won't change his ruling *post hoc*, and he might be even more severe next time around. 'I thought that she did well,' I said.

'Thank you, dear,' Beth said. She was looking from one to the other of us, sensing undercurrents. I was as puzzled. Aubrey Stoneham did not usually mingle with those he regarded as *hoi polloi*. He was working up to something.

'I thought she did very well. Of course, the competition was strong. Sometimes, doing very well isn't enough,' Stoneham said slowly. 'You don't seem to be in very good odour just now. It shouldn't affect the outcome of a trial, but it can do. Judgement between good performances is very subjective, after all.'

A cold hand played scales up and down my back. I thought that I might prefer not to hear any more.

'What do you mean?' Beth asked.

He never took his eyes off me. 'You seem to be making waves on the subject of Lansdyke's wretched dog,' he said. 'And then there's this cruelty thing hanging over you.'

I must have gaped at him like an idiot. My mind refused to find any rational connection. Again, it was Beth who spoke. 'What cruelty thing?'

He glanced at her for the first time. 'Come on, now,' he said. 'You must know.' I was almost convinced that he believed what he was saying.

'No,' Beth said. 'We don't.'

'You weren't aware that a complaint against you is being considered, for unnecessarily brutal treatment of the dogs in your care?'

'That's rubbish,' I said. It had to be. I may give a young dog, at most, one good shake on the first occasion when it decides that the order to 'come' may be disobeyed with impunity. After that, my two guiding principles in training are that a dog should never be tempted to learn the wrong habits and thereafter should be praised for success rather than blamed for failure. I even have to warn a purchaser that punishment may be counter-productive because it may be outside the dog's previous experience.

Stoneham sighed rather theatrically and delved in the pockets of his Goretex coat. He brought out an orange envelope of the kind in which photographic prints are supplied. 'These have only just reached me and I shall want them all back. Before you waste your breath and my time in denials, you'd better look through them.'

There were about ten photographs in the envelope. I glanced at each one before passing it to Beth although after the first two or three my mind refused to accept the evidence of my eyes. Each purported to show me beating a spaniel. I tend to recognise dogs by their mannerisms rather than by their markings, but even so I thought that I could recognise the bitch in the pictures and the place where the impossible acts had occurred. I was too numbed with shock to take in any other details.

Beth spent longer studying the prints. She handed them back to Stoneham. 'They're fakes, of course,' she said.

'You're going to tell me that you've never seen your husband, a professional trainer, raise his hand to a dog?'

'I've seen him raise his hand often enough. But only as a warning. I've never seen him bring it down.'

Stoneham dropped the envelope of prints into his pocket and got to his feet. 'Believe what you want to believe,' he said. 'But I think that you should keep a very low profile for a good long while, both of you.' He nodded and turned away.

Beth was out of her chair before I could stop her. She caught Stoneham by the sleeve. 'Did you shoot Horace?' she demanded.

'Who?'

'Mr Lansdyke's springer.'

I had got to my feet but I lowered myself into

the chair again. It was too late to interfere. People were staring and, if I joined in, I could only make the argument escalate.

Aubrey Stoneham's high colour became more florid even than usual. 'Certainly not,' he said. 'How dare you, young woman? If you're in any doubt, watch the reports in *Gundog World*. A week ago today, wasn't it? I was judging at a retriever stake in the Borders that day. Good evening to you.'

He swung away again and I saw him go out through the hall. Beth came back to our table. 'Go and cancel our room and pay the bill while I pack,' she said. 'We're going home.'

Army life had inured me against emotional shocks but my long illness had lowered my resistance. Perhaps something within me had tried to provide a substitute for that mental fortitude by granting me the gift of sleep in crises. Whatever the cause, sudden worry is followed immediately by all the symptoms of exhaustion. I drove for the first few miles, but as soon as she saw me yawn Beth made me pull into a lay-by while she took over the wheel.

Perhaps I dozed for a while. I certainly have no recollection of the journey between Glasgow and Kinross. Then, quite suddenly, I was alert again.

I wanted to discuss Aubrey Stoneham's bombshell, but Beth cut me short with uncharacteristic abruptness. 'Not just now,' she said. 'I want to think.'

A few years earlier, I would have made a sarcastic retort. Beth's apparent youth and occasional shyness do not suggest the deep thinker, nor is she much given to cogitation. But I had found over the years that when Beth starts to ponder she is not easily turned aside, and she usually arrives at a goal that is eminently logical. So I sat and fretted until I dozed again.

It was after midnight before we turned in at the gates of Three Oaks. I had expected Isobel to be asleep in the spare room, quite possibly pickled although with everything firmly under control. But lights were on in the house and also over at the kennels and it was Henry who emerged from the front door as the car drew up.

He came straight to Beth's window and bent down stiffly. 'Isobel's down with the dogs,' he said. 'Something's happened. We don't understand it and I won't even try to tell you. We phoned the hotel but you'd already left. We guessed that you'd be on the way home. You'd better go and speak to her.'

'Of course,' Beth said. 'We'll have to go down and kennel these two anyway.'

We fetched Jason and Sunbeam out of the car and took them with us. Henry stood and watched us go. It was unlike him to stand aside during a crisis. I tried to imagine what fresh calamity had befallen us.

Between the house and the clusters of kennels was the isolation kennel with its own run. Stardust's season seemed to have been a false heat but her real season was almost due so we were keeping her in the isolation kennel as a precaution. Under the harsh lamp which hung over the run Isobel was seated on the ground, making soothing noises to Stardust. She looked up as we approached.

'Don't come any nearer until you've put those dogs away,' she said urgently. Usually, her first words would have been to ask what awards we'd brought back with us. 'Let John do it.'

I walked on and kennelled Sunbeam and Jason. As I returned, I saw that Beth had walked up to the wire and that Isobel was gently stroking the spaniel bitch but, as I neared, Stardust bolted into the kennel. I stopped where I was, puzzled and hurt. For the first time in my life, a dog had given me a sense of rejection.

'She did the same when Henry came near,' Isobel said. She got up and dusted the skirt of her old tweed coat.

'It's not just me, then,' I said weakly. 'That's a relief.'

'But that's not like Stardust,' Beth said. 'What's come over her?'

'It isn't Stardust,' Isobel said tersely.

# FIVE

'It looked like Stardust,' I said, 'from the brief glimpse I got of her backside.' I groped for a sensible explanation. 'Has one of the other bitches come in season?'

'Not that I know of.' Isobel joined us outside the run. 'When I came out for a last check, I saw that the padlock had disappeared and Stardust seemed to be behaving oddly—'

'Those padlocks are supposed to be unpickable,' Beth protested.

'Anybody with a pair of bolt-cutters could shear one off,' I said. Something in my throat was making speech difficult. 'Weren't the microphones switched on?' The dogs were our best burglar-alarm, so microphones over the kennels were linked to speakers in the house.

'The wires had been cut, Henry says. He joined them up again and taped them, but we'll have to get an electrician.'

'But the wires are underground,' Beth protested.

'They were cut where they go up to come in at the side of the window.'

'We'll have to re-route them to enter the house below ground level,' I said. 'Go on, Isobel.'

'That's about it. I thought she'd had a fright but then I saw that it wasn't the same bitch. She's very similar – I think somebody's added to her markings with a little dye – but I could see small differences straight away. She was nervous of me but she let me examine her. It was very peculiar and worrying so I phoned Henry and he came straight over, but his presence terrified her. She seems to be all right with women but she's terrified of men. Some man's ill-used her. There are marks . . .'

'Why on earth would somebody substitute one bitch for another?' I asked.

'Perhaps he'd ruined one bitch and decided to start over again.'

'No,' Beth said loudly. We waited. 'It's all of a piece,' she said more quietly. 'We've had our own excitements. Let's go inside before John gets frozen. And we haven't had anything to eat since a couple of sandwiches at lunchtime.'

Henry was waiting in the hall. 'Well?' he said.

'The same with John as with you,' Isobel told him.

'Hell!'

The large kitchen was warm, with the boiler muttering away in one corner, but its bright and cheerful aspect seemed to have fled. Beth, still in her sheepskin coat, sat me down at the table and heated canned soup in the microwave. While I nursed the hot mug in my hands and told Isobel and Henry about Aubrey Stoneham's hints and the photographs, things began to sizzle in a frying pan.

'The photographs are fakes, of course,' Beth told Isobel. 'Do you and Henry want to eat with us?'

'Yes, of course they are,' Isobel said. 'I wouldn't be in any doubt of that. And yes, that smells too good to pass up. Henry?'

Henry nodded.

'Have mine,' I said. The soup was warming and comforting but I was sure that I would never eat again.

'Nonsense,' Henry said briskly. 'You'll eat what's put in front of you or Beth will feed you through a tube, and you know it. Are we to assume that the po-faced Stoneham was warning you off looking into the shooting of Horace?'

'He didn't put it in so many words,' Beth said. 'In fact, I think he chose his words rather carefully. But that's what he meant.'

Henry raised his eyebrows. 'A shot spaniel and one that's been abused, surely there has to be a connection. The faking of photographs and the substitution of a dog seems rather drastic in the circumstances. And the shooting incident only happened a week ago. Your questions, John, could hardly have come to the notice of Horace's would-be assassin before early to middle of this week. Not much time for such an elaborate plot and no time at all to find a dog resembling Stardust and reduce it to a state of terror. How good were the photographs?'

'I sneaked one of them into my pocket,' Beth

said. 'I'll show you in a minute.' She began to serve bacon, eggs and kidneys onto plates. 'There was just one good photograph of John, raising his hand as if to give Dusty a slap – you know how he does.' (Dusty was Beth's occasional pet-name for Stardust.) 'It's only a pretence and even the dogs don't take it seriously. That one was sharp and clear and it seemed to be on slightly different paper from the others. I couldn't be sure, but I think it was taken at a Sunday Masterclass. The rest were like this.'

She put a photograph into Isobel's hands and then resumed serving the food. It had been a long time since our sandwich lunch and the soup had brought my hunger back in a rush of saliva.

'But this could be anybody,' Isobel said. 'And almost anywhere.'

Beth sat down with her own plate and picked up her fork. 'That's what I mean,' she said. 'A man with a build something like John's, wearing a Barbour coat, jeans and Wellies and one of those fits-all-sizes caps, just as John was in the one good photograph. You never see his face again, but he's laying into a spaniel that could be mistaken for Stardust. I suppose it's that bitch out there.

'So look at it this way round. Somebody wonders what sort of leverage he could get on us. He remembers that he has the original photograph available or knows where he can get a print of it. And suppose that he knows of somebody who's been beating a spaniel. He gets a pal to pose in the act of giving it another hiding, or even does it himself if his camera has a delay. Then he waits for a chance to plant the dog on us. He may have had a choice of dogs, because I remember John demonstrating his training methods and putting several of them through their paces. He picked on Dusty because she was in one of the original photographs and the substitute bitch looked most like her. It was just his luck that she was in the isolation kennel because of her season.' She took her first mouthful. 'This food's cold,' she said indignantly. She got up to reheat it in the microwave oven.

'I was going to move her back among the others when her false season ended,' Isobel said. 'It didn't seem worthwhile, when she's so damned irregular. If she'd been in her usual kennel, the presence of a stranger would have set them all off. I'd probably have heard that, with or without the microphones.'

'I doubt it,' I said. The house was solidly built and double glazed.

My appetite had flagged again. I pushed my plate away. Beth pushed it back at me. 'Take a look at the background,' she said.

I was studying the photograph more closely than I had done at the hotel. 'Grass, part of the trunk of an oak and a lot of sky,' I said, 'and mostly out of focus. This was taken from closer than the one that really is of me.'

'And I'll tell you why,' Beth said. 'So that there wouldn't be much background. The original photograph, the genuine one, was taken in the summer. The photographer came in closer this time so as not to show any detail of the tree and also so that the lack of leaves on the tree wouldn't show. The original photograph would only make the fakes look authentic if they all seem to have been taken at the same time and place.' She picked up her fork and resumed eating.

Henry placed his cutlery neatly on his empty plate. 'There must be more going on than we know about so far,' he said. 'I still think that it's too much trouble and risk – let alone giving away a potentially valuable dog – for anyone to go to over peppering somebody else's spaniel, a shooting that could possibly have been passed off as an accident in the field. An apology and an offer to pay the vet's bill would usually be enough. Unless, of course, there's somebody who's absolutely dependent on Arthur Lansdyke's goodwill. When do you speak to him again?' he asked Isobel.

'I expect him to phone tomorrow. I could ask him who'd have most to lose by angering him.'

'Yes, do,' Beth said. 'What other steps can we take?'

'None,' I said. I pushed my plate away again.

I was surprised to notice that I had almost finished it.

This time, Beth let me leave the remainder. 'You mean that we lie down and play dead?'

'If you want to put it that way. Stoneham didn't only make a threat. He also showed us that a hostile judge can take away our just awards. Our reputation, and the prices we can ask, depend on our success in trials. That's one side of it. The other is that a scandal about cruel training methods would ruin us. We have some friends who'd refuse to believe it, but not many of the dog-owning public know us as well as that. Just imagine the effect of a prosecution by the SSPCA and denunciation in the tabloids.

'We know that that poor beast out there isn't Stardust; but how do we prove it to those who don't know her as intimately as we do? I don't think that any really detailed and authenticated photographs of her exist.'

'She appears once or twice among groups of dogs in the sporting magazines,' Isobel said, 'but I wouldn't expect anyone to identify her from one of those. Could we try genetic fingerprinting?'

'We don't have Stardust and she hasn't had pups,' I pointed out. 'Her sire was put down last year and her dam's been taken abroad. We'd have to get tissue from several of her siblings. We could only find them through the Kennel Club. God knows who'd learn what we were up to. We could provoke the very disaster that we're hoping to avoid. And we'd be out of business long before I could clear myself.' I nearly added that genetic fingerprints cost nearly two hundred quid each but I stopped myself. I had a nasty feeling that money was going to be no object by the time the crisis was over. Henry and Isobel considered me to be a skinflint; but they had money and no dependants while I had a shred of a pension and I was still hoping that dependants would come along some day.

'But that means leaving Stardust in the hands of whoever took her,' Beth protested.

I shrugged.

'What John doesn't want to say aloud,' Henry put in, 'is that Stardust may very well be dead and buried by now.'

Beth turned white and blinked several times. 'But there must be something we can do,' she said bravely. 'Couldn't we strike first? Get Mr Hautry over from the SSPCA, show him the bitch and explain about the fake photographs? Then, if the photographs ever did surface, he wouldn't take them at face value.'

'He might just think that *Qui s'excuse s'accuse*,' Henry said.

'He could see that that isn't one of our oak trees,' Beth said doggedly.

Henry picked up the photograph again. 'I'm not sure that he could. It's too fuzzy. Perhaps you should get rid of the changeling.'

'Put her down, you mean?' Beth asked indignantly.

'Not necessarily. Board her out, somewhere a long way away.'

'If that ever came out, it would look much worse,' I said. I was so tired that I was holding my eyelids up by conscious willpower. 'Do whatever you like, just as long as you can be absolutely sure that word of it can't get back to whoever faked those photographs.'

Beth had to help me to my feet. I stumbled upstairs.

## SIX

I was sure that I had fallen asleep in my clothes and on top of the duvet. I seemed to sleep like the dead but I was aware of Beth's restlessness beside me. When I awoke, in my pyjamas and inside the bed, she was gone and a cup of tea was cooling beside the bed clothes. This was not unusual. I had slept late, by our standards. Sometimes my sleep was light and I was up and about before dawn. If I slept in, Beth would slip away and leave me.

When I arrived downstairs, I found that the chores had been done meticulously and my breakfast had been laid on the kitchen table. Although Isobel often took Sundays off, she had stayed the night as planned and was exercising the puppies on the lawn. I guessed that she would find it difficult to stay away while a threat was hanging over us. Beth had disappeared in my car.

Toying with breakfast, I found that during the night my thoughts had come together. I tried to arrange them in logical sequence. Life would have to go on until the axe fell. I would have to resume my constant training programme with the older dogs, but there was one task which seemed to be more urgent. The unpleasant Mr Stoneham had conveyed to us, from an unknown source, a threat of dire consequences unless we refrained from asking further questions. Those consequences would spell ruin and so, I had decided, investigation was at an end. But we were stuck with a spaniel bitch, resembling the now absent Stardust but with a fear of men. That fear might prove to be the strongest evidence against us. The wisest course might, as Henry had hinted, have been a large injection of tranquilliser and a quiet burial in the night, although I knew that none of us would have the heart for so ruthless an action. But our unknown enemy would neither know nor care if we did our best for our visitor; indeed, he would expect nothing else. He might even want the bitch back some day – but that, I was determined, would be quite another story.

I filled my coat pockets with a variety of the sort of titbits that dogs crave, picked up a low fishing stool from my junk room and went out into the cool, damp air of early winter. Isobel seemed to be fully occupied in teaching a young pup to retrieve a rolled-up sock, so I passed her by.

Somebody had taken a spare padlock out of store, set it to our standard combination and locked the isolation kennel. Some ill-disposed person had carried off one of our padlocks and if he cared to dismantle it with a hacksaw he might well be able to discover the setting. The padlocks had been chosen, at a hellish cost, because the combinations could be reset and it would be only sensible to reset the whole lot. But that would have to wait. I let myself into the wire mesh run.

The wooden kennel – with metal corners to prevent chewing – formed the end wall of the run. There was no sign of the bitch except for small rustlings inside the kennel. If she had made use of the run for sanitary purposes, Beth had cleaned up the traces. I seated myself where she would at least see my hands through the low, open doorway and began to speak to her in the most soothing voice I could manage.

There was absolute silence from inside the kennel.

We needed a name for the visitor, but names were in short supply. A consistent theme both helps to identify the strain from a particular kennel and makes the choosing of individual names less contentious. Our purchases of breeding stock had, of course, already been named and registered, while young puppies were usually named by their buyers. But, stemming from my two bitches who had begun the strain, the spaniels we bred and raised had been given kennel-names derived from the light and shade of the sun, moon and stars. Names originating from fire were usually reserved for males although Lucy had begun life as Lucifer. (Henry's suggestions, which had included Taillight and Foglamp, had been shouted down.)

We had more or less decided to switch to the world of horticulture. Reference to the gardening books suggested that there were more than enough names to supply us indefinitely. We considered naming the dogs after trees and the bitches after flowers; but I broke that rule before it was introduced by calling the new bitch Walnut, for no reason that my conscious mind could perceive.

After some minutes of this one-sided conversation, the small noises resumed as Walnut began to relax; but I did not hear the patting sound that a dog's tail makes in response to a friendly voice.

Still speaking gently, although I was hard put to it to find anything to say, I opened my penknife and cut up an apple. I reached as far as I could into the kennel and placed a segment of apple on the clean floor, adding a biscuit and a piece of chocolate. There was no immediate reaction, but a minute or two later I heard a stir inside the kennel and, when I leaned down to look, the biscuit and the chocolate had disappeared.

If she did not like apple, so be it. Without interrupting my now laboured chatter, I ate the rest of the apple myself.

Three biscuits later, by which time I was giving Walnut my considered views about the situation in the Middle East, I decided to try for another step forward. I pushed my hand in as far as I could with a biscuit on the palm, still chatting as comfortably as I could from my cramped position and trying not to remember that a nervous snatch could cost me some skin. After several minutes and just before my aching muscles forced me to give up, I was rewarded by a soft snuffle and the tickle of whiskers as the biscuit was lifted from my hand.

That was as much progress as I could expect in a single visit. I left my stool where it was, locked the gate of the run and backed away. On the off-chance, I waited twenty yards off. Soon, a face appeared at the kennel door. She came far enough out to sniff my fishing stool and then retired to lie with her head just inside the door, watching me unblinkingly. She was very similar to Stardust although her nose was fractionally shorter and I thought that there was something different about the eyes. I produced my last biscuit and held it up where she could see it.

There was a danger that I could frighten her again if she had been subjected to stone-throwing, but gentle throwing motions caused no more than a slight twitching. I tossed the biscuit as gently as I could and it landed in the run. The face vanished immediately but reappeared. I retired a few more paces and she ventured out, picked up the biscuit and retired quickly.

Breathing a sigh of relief, I turned towards the house.

While I was preoccupied with Walnut, my car had returned. It was standing at the nearest point of the gravel and two figures were coming slowly across the grass. I was surprised to recognise the elderly kilted figure of Charles Buccleugh. He was leaning on a stick and also on the arm of Henry who, although not a member of the partnership, often walked over to give Isobel his company and us his help and advice. On this occasion, after all the midnight activity, I guessed that he had stayed overnight with Isobel and slept in even later than I had. Beth, who had been locking up the car, avoided my eye and scuttled indoors.

The two elders halted as I neared them and we exchanged greetings. 'Your delightful young wife came to invite me over for a look around your kennels,' Buccleugh said. 'I was glad of an excuse to be around spaniels again for a while and also to get out of the house. My daughter has the Ellingworth brats with her for the day,

71

nice enough lasses but an old man can take just so much exuberant young girlhood. Beth – she asked me to call her Beth – also told me about your present problem.' He saw that I was dumbfounded and smiled softly. 'She was careful to ask first whether I had become friendly with Aubrey Stoneham and I was able to assure her that my attitude was unchanged. It seems that, on a previous occasion, her then employer was called away suddenly to stand in at a trial, because somebody had fallen ill and I had refused point blank to be a co-judge with Stoneham. I remember the occasion. I had shared the duty with him previously and found him prepared to overlook failures by his friends and determined to persuade his colleague to do likewise. After what I said on that occasion, we never spoke again. So you can trust my discretion.'

'I'm sure we can,' I said weakly.

Henry winked at me. 'Shall we move on? I'm sure Mr Buccleugh would be happy to get the inspection over and to sit down.' We moved towards the kennels, taking our pace from Buccleugh. 'Beth,' Henry went on, 'may also have been influenced by the fact that Mr Buccleugh still knows most of the dog world, including who is and who is not friendly towards the unspeakable Stoneham. And, because you visited him after the first incident, he has an excuse to ask questions about the shooting of

Horace on his own account, without compromising this establishment.'

'Ah,' Buccleugh said. 'That would no doubt explain why we arrived here by a somewhat roundabout route.'

'To avoid having you seen in her company. One would suppose so,' Henry said. 'Our young friend here thinks that his wife is impetuous, but in my experience she thinks things out very carefully before she acts.'

'I have the same impression,' Buccleugh said.

The two old gentlemen nodded in unison. They had not met before but they seemed to have struck up an instant rapport.

We toured very slowly round the kennels. Buccleugh was complimentary about our setup and our dogs. He had a remarkable memory and it was evident that he still kept up with the trial results, because he was able to recite the awards, some of the pedigrees and even most of the unplaced runs of each of our trialling dogs.

On our way back towards the house, we paused not far from the isolation kennel. 'May I see your changeling?' Buccleugh asked.

'If she'll come out,' I said. I walked forward to within a dozen paces of the pen and whistled softly. There was a rustle from inside the kennel and a pair of eyes gleamed. Then a face showed in the opening. I spoke to her and let her see one of my last two pieces of chocolate and then lobbed it into the run. After a cautious look around, she came out and gobbled. This time, instead of darting back under cover, she stood in the open, poised for a quick retreat.

The others had come slowly up beside me. 'May I see if I can get closer?' Buccleugh asked.

'Try, by all means,' I said, handing him my last piece of chocolate.

Without Henry's supporting arm, he was very slow. The arthritis was evidently troubling him. But he shuffled closer, making chirruping noises and leaning heavily on his stick, and to my surprise the bitch stood her ground, eventually taking the chocolate from his fingers.

Buccleugh turned with a triumphant grin. 'They always know who are their true friends,' he said. 'Could I have an arm again, please?'

As soon as Henry stepped forward, Walnut vanished into the kennel. 'I was hoping that I might see a clue to her breeding,' Buccleugh said, 'but no such luck. A nice-looking bitch, though. If you can get the pedigree, you might do worse than breed from her.'

'I'd want to see her working first,' I said.

'And have her hips and eyes checked. Of course.' Despite the lines of pain on his face, I could see that he was pleased with himself and also amused.

'Come clean,' Henry said to him, offering his arm. 'You've got some idea in your head as to why she let you approach and not either of us.'

'True,' Buccleugh said. He hobbled a few

more paces. 'It's only a wild guess, but worth a try. Does either of you have a kilt?'

'We each do,' I said. Mine was intended for evening wear, bought in a rash and affluent moment and rarely worn, but Henry was often to be seen in a kilt of the yellow McLeod tartan.

'I suggest that you try wearing it. I remember when a kennel-maid, some years ago, took to giving my dogs a dunt with the broom whenever they got in her way. Several dogs took against women after that. Dogs don't depend on their eyes as much as their other senses, but their viewpoint is at trouser level. If she's been treated gently by a woman and harshly by one or more men, she may be associating trousers with assault.'

'A good point!' Henry said. 'I'll dash home later and change. Then I can take over the attempt at therapy and let John get on with the real work of the kennels.'

'That would help,' I admitted, 'although it may be more important to get her reconciled to me than to you. I'm the one who's being accused.'

We were almost at the front door. 'Of course,' Buccleugh said, 'nobody has asked me to help in so many words. But—'

'We'd be more than grateful for any help you can give us,' I said.

He ignored my words although I thought that there was a smile at the back of his old eyes. 'But, if they should do so, the temptation to escape for a while from the monotony of my invalid existence and the company of Ellingworth's progeny, and at the same time to rock Aubrey Stoneham's boat for him, would be irresistible.'

'Don't try to resist it,' Henry said. 'What use is temptation if you don't give in to it?'

'He's lived his life on that principle,' I told Buccleugh, 'and it doesn't seem to have done him any harm.'

Evidently Beth classed Charles Buccleugh in the very uppermost rank of visitors, at least as high as Lord Crail and considerably higher than any of our few relatives. Coffee and buttered scones were waiting in the sitting-room, which was rarely used so early in the day except on special occasions. The vase of dried beech-leaves had been removed from the fireplace to the side-table and a log fire burned in the grate, counteracting the central heating by drawing cold air into the room but creating a picture of warmth and comfort.

Charles Buccleugh paused to admire our one good picture which hung over the fireplace before lowering himself carefully into one of the wing-chairs. Henry, by virtue of age, took the other. Isobel joined us. She and I sat in the settee and Beth, after a doubtful look at me, settled between us.

'It's all right,' I said. I felt her relax. 'I know

that I said that we'd keep our heads down, but you're right. We have to do something, just as long as we're very, very cautious. We can't just wait for the sword to fall. So what do you think?' I asked Buccleugh.

He accepted a cup of coffee and a biscuit, stirring thoughtfully. 'For a start,' he said at last, 'I quite accept your version of events. I've had the binoculars on you often enough while you've been training dogs on Easter Colm and I've never seen you give one of them even a flick with the lead. The photograph that I saw in the car – may I see it again?' Beth handed it to him. He took out a spectacle case and removed a pair of gold-rimmed half-glasses. 'That's better! This, as Beth told me repeatedly, could be of almost anybody; but taken together with a better shot of you in the apparent act of beating a dog, it would be damning. It might not stand up as evidence in a court, but the eyes of the press and public are what you have to fear.

'Next, your wife' – he gave Beth a nod which was almost a bow – 'told me that you wanted to keep your heads down – your own, military, expression – and be seen to do nothing. She was quite indignant about it, but I think you're right. You need the utmost caution. The threat's a serious one. The kind of publicity hanging over you would ruin you. I still have some clout with the Kennel Club and a little with the SSPCA, but if the tabloids were making a stishie about it my voice would count for nothing. And a scandal about cruelty to animals, and in an establishment catering to the shooting fraternity, would be meat and drink to the popular press. Your only recourse might be a libel action which would cost the earth, take for ever and which you might not win. And even if you came out on top, it would be the original slur which the public remembered.

'On the other hand, as Henry pointed out, you could hardly be put at risk if I were to do some inquiring, my curiosity inflamed by your visit of last week – if by any chance my inquiries came to the ears of your enemy, which I don't think they would.'

'Exactly,' Henry said. 'It seems to me that your only course, John, if you're not going to sit still and hope for the best, is to find out who's behind this and why. So let's consider what we know about him. Or her or them, but let's assume that he's singular and male for the moment.'

'But we don't know a damn thing about him,' I said.

Buccleugh smiled at me encouragingly. 'Don't despair so easily,' he said. 'My guess is that you'll find that you know much more than you think you do. Let me make a few suggestions. Some of these points are inferences and may prove wrong. For instance, you infer that he has something to fear from Arthur Lansdyke. That seems speculative. There could be many other reasons why he didn't want it generally known that he shot spaniels.

'But he has a connection with Aubrey Stoneham or a hold over him – if the culprit isn't Stoneham himself. Stoneham lent his weight to the pressure on you, perhaps believing innocently in the evidence, perhaps wanting to believe it.

'Next, he obtained the original, genuine photograph. Ask yourselves how he came by it.'

'John runs what we call his Masterclass once a month,' Beth said. 'There are always cameras clicking away. People like to record the progress their dogs make. And if somebody wanted a photograph that somebody else had taken of his own dog, he'd be as likely to borrow the negatives of the whole film.'

'And have them printed,' Henry said. 'It's difficult to pick out one dog in a strip of negatives.'

'That's true,' Buccleugh said. 'So, a possible connection with somebody who's attended the Masterclass. And then, he has a camera, or the use of one. And access to a darkroom.'

'Why a darkroom?' Isobel asked.

Buccleugh flicked the photograph impatiently. 'This isn't the sort of material you'd put through your local chemist. There have been prosecutions in the past because some technician in a photographic lab spotted pornographic or illegal material. Suppose that one of the technicians was

79

a dog-lover. He'd be round to the SSPCA in two jumps.'

Isobel threw up her hands. 'Question answered,' she said.

Again Buccleugh gave a nod which was almost a bow. 'Next, the bitch. Did I hear you address her as Walnut?'

'Just a name I plucked out of the air,' I said. 'I don't know why. I felt that I had to start giving her back an identity.'

'Let her be Walnut, then. Walnut wasn't imprinted with that deep fear of men in the day or two that was available to him.'

'More than a day or two, surely,' I said.

Buccleugh looked at me benignly. 'The questions you asked of Lansdyke's neighbours were natural. After that, you would have been expected to let the matter drop. I think that the visit here of a policeman, or your trip to Kilcolm in his company, made somebody believe that you were pushing your inquiries further. It put the wind up him. Even I, in my ivory tower, heard gossip about it.'

'But that was about something totally different.'

'Our quarry might not know that. What he did know was where he could put his hand on a springer bitch, already a nervous wreck and bearing at least a passing resemblance to the one in the original photograph.'

'You're drawing heavily on coincidence, aren't you?' Isobel said.

'Not if you look at it from the other side,' Henry said. 'As Beth pointed out, it may have been the availability of the photographs and the dog that put the plan into his mind. Other circumstances might have generated a different plan.'

The logical progress of the two wise old boys was giving me heart. The atmosphere in the room seemed to be brightening. I decided to add my own small contribution. 'He knew enough about this place to be able to neutralise our alarm system.'

Buccleugh nodded approvingly. 'Perhaps from his visit to the Masterclass. He had access to a shotgun and a mixed lot of cartridges. What else?'

We drank coffee in contemplative silence for most of a minute. 'I think that's all,' I said.

Charles Buccleugh shook his head at me. Evidently I had disappointed him. 'There remains the one question to which we can only guess the answer. He had a motive for shooting the dog. If the dog had, for instance, been raiding Mr Ellingworth's chicken-house, Ellingworth rather than Mr Lansdyke would have been the aggrieved party. So why the desperate efforts to avert any inquiries? When we know that, we'll know it all.'

'Mr Lansdyke phoned this morning,' Isobel

said. 'I had no good news for him about Horace. He couldn't suggest anyone who'd have a reason to worry about his good will.

Charles Buccleugh began to struggle up from the chair. 'If Mrs Cunningham will run me home, I'll start phoning around.'

'Do it from here,' I said. 'Stay to lunch.'

'Thank you, but no. Another time, perhaps. At home, I have a book of phone-numbers an inch thick. Meanwhile, you should spend time with Walnut. It's amazing how much a dog can tell you, if you have understanding.'

Beth and I took an arm each and helped him to his feet. 'We'll be more than happy to pay your next phone-bill,' I said.

He chuckled, a rattling sound from deep in his chest. 'No need for that. I've been waiting for an excuse to call up some old friends. And reclaim a few favours. As I may have said before, life gets very boring when you're old and a cripple.' We had almost reached the door, but he stopped and turned round carefully. 'I'm not afraid of that word,' he said. 'I'm trying to come to terms with what life is doing to me. I am a cripple, not a "disabled person". I don't know why we start off with perfectly good words for human conditions and bodily functions and then decide that the words, because of their meaning, must themselves be unacceptable. Then we find it necessary to invent coy and unwieldy euphemisms. The world is becoming mealy-mouthed. How long before those euphemisms themselves become unacceptable in their turn?'

I helped him into the car and watched Beth drive off.

Henry was alone in the sitting-room. 'A forthright old boy,' he said. 'I like that. I hope I'll be able to face my declining years with the same courage. Tell me, why Walnut? You'd better have a good explanation ready when Beth asks you why you chose that name.'

'I plucked it out of the air. I told you.'

'You plucked it out of your subconscious. "A woman, a spaniel and a walnut tree,"' he quoted, '"the more you beat them, the better they be."'

'If you look it up, I think you'll find that the original referred to an ass, not a spaniel. And don't you forget it,' I added more cheerfully. It was not often that I could bandy quotations with Henry.

Henry decided to walk home, change into his kilt and grab a pub lunch on the way back. I put in an hour, taking the older dogs out of their kennels one by one and putting them through their basic exercises. A bolting rabbit furnishes the most testing temptation for a gun dog but our rabbit-pen had been visited by myxomatosis. I spent some time on steadiness training, using a rabbit-skin dummy powered by shock-cord.

Walnut might by now be ready to accept another dose of sympathetic treatment. Hurrying her along might have its dangers, but the scandal might break at any time. I changed into my own kilt with the bare minimum of accessories, accepted the snack that Beth forced on me, filled my sporran with more chocolates and biscuits, put a brush in my jacket pocket and approached the isolation kennel making soothing noises. This time, the black and white face remained visible in the shadows. A biscuit tossed into the run from a few yards away was accepted, but when I entered the pen she retired again into the kennel.

I sat down again on my stool and reached inside with a biscuit.

Ten minutes and several titbits later, we began to make real progress. A biscuit was lifted gently off my palm and Walnut's moist nose stayed just within my reach. When I stroked it I felt her tense, ready for a quick withdrawal, and then relax. Her tongue flicked once over my knuckles.

It must have been touch and go which ran out first – her timidity, my patience or her stomach capacity. I sat and coaxed her until my muscles ached and my legs were numb under me, but with each morsel she allowed herself to be persuaded nearer to the doorway and let me stroke a little more of her head and neck until she suddenly made up her mind and moved, to lie half out of the door, her head on her forepaws and her eyes rolled up to watch me.

Very slowly, I extricated the brush from my pocket and began to groom her coat. She flinched at the first touch but remained where she was. Being brushed is a sensation few dogs can resist, a pleasure in itself and a signal of family membership. Walnut inched further out so that I could reach the unscratchable area of her lower back. She left me in no doubt that bruising here and there still troubled her but already she trusted me to work carefully around her bruises, contenting herself with a subdued squeak if I found another tender spot. I brushed gently, keeping up the soothing words. The gloss began to come back to her coat. She was a sturdy and, as Buccleugh had said, an attractive spaniel with soft eyes and a gentle nature. I wondered what kind of a man could bring himself to ill-treat her.

'Amazing!' said Henry's voice. I looked up. Magnificently kilted in the tartan of the McLeods, he was watching us from a distance, puffing luxuriously on a cheroot.

'Come and make her acquaintance,' I said.

Henry walked towards the wire mesh of the run. When he was still a few yards off I felt Walnut tense. An instant later, I was alone in the run.

'What did I do?' Henry asked plaintively. 'Doesn't she like my tartan?'

'Nobody likes that tartan,' I said. 'But I don't think it's that. As your even older friend pointed out, they can recognise a villain a mile off.' But then I relented. Henry was only trying to help. 'He also said that it's amazing what a dog can tell you, if you can read the language. I suggest you get rid of that cigar. Then go into the house and wash away all trace of the smell while I start again from Square One. We may learn something.'

When Henry returned, still grumbling that the tartan had been good enough for his mother's ancestors, Walnut was once again outside the kennel and submitting to brushing. The smell of the cheroot must still have been clinging to his clothes because, although she suffered his approach, she would not stay in the pen with him.

'That seems conclusive,' I said. 'And you know as well as I do that all the modern tartans were the inventions of Victorians who wanted to cut a dash. Let's go into the house.'

There was time for one further check. Isobel, an occasional smoker, had some cigarettes in her handbag. We sent her down to discover Walnut's reaction to cigarette smoke. Isobel returned to say that the spaniel had seemed, if anything, to enjoy it.

Beth phoned Charles Buccleugh to tell him that Walnut's assailant had been a cigar smoker, but that the woman who had treated her more gently had probably smoked cigarettes.

# SEVEN

There was wind in the night and when I woke on Monday morning the clouds had blown away, leaving cold sunshine and a brisk breeze.

I spent a few minutes after breakfast, consolidating my friendship with Walnut. But the routine work of a busy breeding and training kennel could not be shelved for long. Our field-trial hopefuls were in danger of getting rusty. For a crash course in steadiness to the sequence of the flush of a bird, a shot and a fall, I use another of my dummies with a pair of wings attached and my length of shock-cord pulled up to a high branch. I was digging the necessary bits and pieces out of my junk-room when Isobel, who was already labouring over the paperwork, called me into the house.

We joined Beth, who had finished the first phase of the chores and returned to the kitchen to prepare the puppies' feed. After squatting beside the isolation kennel, I was glad to settle for a minute in one of the basket chairs before all the walking that a day of dog-training entails. Isobel sat at the kitchen table, typing letters in answer to the inquiries that our last advertisement had brought in. The office, as we liked to call it, was far too small for more than the storage of records and was also isolated from the social hub.

'Charles Buccleugh was on the phone,' Isobel said.

'Already?'

'He doesn't have many other calls on his time,' she pointed out. 'He says that he picked up one or two hints about dog-abuse yesterday, but nothing that he could confirm. He had to leave it until this morning, when people were back in their offices. He got hold of an old friend, now a big wheel in the SSPCA.' She saw me look up. 'Don't get your hopes too high,' she said quickly. 'Charles doesn't think that he could do more than put in a good word, if the accusation is ever made. But he knows this chap well enough to check out the few names he'd accumulated. Most of them were non-starters – wrong breed, or dog destroyed, that sort of thing.

'He's left with one hopeful one. If a dog's being knocked about, it doesn't keep quiet about it and there's usually a complaint; so, if this isn't the source, Walnut must come from a very long way away or from somewhere too far out in the country for the neighbours to hear a dog yelping.

'There was a complaint to the SSPCA, about a month ago, about a man beating a spaniel bitch, variety unspecified. A William Randall.' She named a small village near Anstruther. 'An SSPCA inspector called. Only a woman was at home. The bitch was nervous but didn't seem to be carrying more marks than a spaniel can pick up working in thick cover. He had more urgent reports to follow up, so he decided that there was inadequate evidence and left it at that.'

'Was the inspector wearing the kilt?' I asked.

'Charles says that he asked that question. His friend said that, knowing that particular inspector, probably yes. And it was the owner's wife who showed him the dog. Charles doesn't know anybody in that area and he seems to have come to a dead end. He's asking whether we know anybody near there. I don't. And I phoned Henry and he doesn't either.'

'Nor do I,' I said. 'So where do we go from here without rocking the boat?'

'I think you do know somebody,' Beth said. 'I sorted out the telephone drawer the other day. You had a change-of-address card about a year ago. I'll fetch it.' She scuttled out of the room.

'Damned if I know who that could be,' I said.

'You're about to find out,' Isobel said absently. She was peering through her glasses at a letter in a faint and spiky handwriting. 'This man says he's looking for a cooker. I suppose he means a cocker.'

Beth came back and dropped a slip of paper in front of me. It seemed to have been churned out from a word processor.

'It's from a Gordon Hemmeling,' Beth said helpfully.

'I'd forgotten all about it. He used to live

somewhere near Bo'ness. Did we send him a Christmas card?'

'Yes. But I did the envelope for you.'

'That's probably why it didn't register,' I said. 'Gordon was an old army pal. He was invalided out at about the same time that I was.'

'You'd better go and see him,' Isobel said. 'Do you know what questions to ask him?'

'I'm not stupid,' I said indignantly. 'We want to know all about this – what was his name again?'

'William Randall,' Isobel said patiently. 'You also want to know if he has any connection with Aubrey Stoneham or anybody else around these parts.'

'Of course I do,' I said. 'But I don't know that Gordon would be able to tell me about that.'

'Perhaps not by name,' Isobel agreed. 'If you had photographs you could at least ask him whether any of those people had been seen with Randall."

It seemed that I was stupid after all. 'But we don't have any photographs. Or do we?' I added.

This time, Beth had no rabbit to pull out of a hat. She shook her head.

'Sending somebody to fool around with a Polaroid would be too dangerous,' Isobel said. 'It might provoke the very reaction we're trying to prevent. The local papers might have something. Henry knows somebody on the *Fife Herald*, but the last thing we could afford would be to make the press curious. You'll have to make do with one of your scurrilous word-pictures for the moment. If that isn't enough, you may have to fetch your friend over here and introduce him around.'

I got up to reach the wall-phone, dialled Gordon Hemmeling and sank back into my chair. Gordon was loudly pleased to hear my voice. I explained that I wanted to come and see him, on a matter so confidential that I would prefer my face to be seen as little as possible.

'Drive right in and up to the garage door,' he said. 'I'll leave the side door unlocked for you. Dive straight inside. When are you coming?'

'Straight away,' I told him. 'If that's all right?'

'Right as rain,' he said. 'We'll talk when you arrive.'

He gave me precise directions and we disconnected.

'You'd better have something to eat before you go,' Beth said.

'Unless Gordon's a changed man he'll be in the kitchen by now, preparing the fatted calf.'

'Don't let him give you a lot of drink if you're driving.' Beth looked at me anxiously. 'Would you like me to come and drive?'

'It'll take him less than an hour each way,' Isobel said. 'He can surely hold together for that long.'

'I suppose so,' Beth said. She was looking doubtful. My illness had given her several frights and she always expected disaster if I was out of her sight for more than a few minutes.

'You'll almost pass the door of the Speer's Wood Kennels,' Isobel said. 'Drop the cocker spaniel letter off with them. They had a litter of them last month.'

Gordon would have pulled my leg unmercifully if I had turned up in a kilt. I changed into slacks before driving off.

A stiff breeze was chasing whitecaps down the estuary of the Forth but the village was sheltered in a broad hollow running down to a bay where, despite the lateness of the season, several boats were dancing at anchor. Following Gordon's directions, I found his house just where he had said it would be, a rambling bungalow, stone-fronted but roughcast at the sides, set in at least half an acre of designer garden. I drove up to the garage and ducked in at the side door without being seen by anyone other than some gulls and a girl on a pony.

Gordon limped through to escort me back to his living-room. He had lost part of his right foot to a left-over mine in the Falklands at about the time when I had been transferred from those islands and was being bitten by an infected leech in Central America.

Physically, we had both changed in the intervening years. My illness had left me so underweight as to be a worry to Beth and my doctor while Gordon, who had always enjoyed his victuals but could no longer take the exercise needed to control the flesh, was now distinctly tubby. He had also cultivated a set of whiskers which the army would never have tolerated since about the time of Gallipoli. He was now, I remembered, a moderately successful writer of historical romances; but he was rumoured also to write, under a female nom de plume, rather more modern and torrid romances of a distinctly voluptuous character. There seemed to be no shortage of money; but his disability pension plus the earnings of a working wife must have amplified very comfortably his royalties as a writer.

The house was at the very end of the main street of the village, beyond the T-junction with the road, so that the living-room window had a view down the street and across the Forth to where the Isle of May lay like a stranded whale. The room was uncluttered and expensively equipped with the latest and best in hide-covered furniture; but a mismatched table was set up in the window, complete with a word-processor and untidy stacks of books and paper. Gordon had a study at the rear of the house, he told me, but he preferred to work where the passing scene could trigger ideas or, at least, let him know that the real and modern world was still around him.

On another table, coffee was already percolating and several calorie-laden cakes were waiting. It was my chance, under Gordon's gluttonous influence, to please Beth by putting back a little weight. Perversely, my appetite declined. I nibbled a biscuit while we talked, remembering old friends now dead or in the higher ranks and wild days long past. We exchanged grumbles about the disasters that had ended our service careers. Gordon was quite willing to discuss his historical books but flatly denied writing anything else.

'But you didn't come here to accuse me of writing soft porn, nor so that we could gossip like a pair of wives across a garden fence,' he said suddenly. 'And I've seen that look before, of a cat waiting for its moment to pounce. Let's put you out of your misery. How can I help you?'

'How well do you know your neighbours?' I asked him.

'Not as well as I should,' he said thoughtfully. 'I spend too much time in here. Writing's a solitary business. And people tend to treat the writer as an alien creature, probably an intellectual and certain to suck them dry and spit them out as a character in a book. They talk, guardedly, but they don't get close. They watch me and I observe them and we each get a certain amount of amusement out of it. Does that disappoint you?'

'Not in the least. You know about them without being intimate. So I can ask you questions – in absolute confidence?'

'Ask away. Who about?'

'One William Randall. Is he a friend of yours?'

Gordon's expression told me the answer before he opened his mouth. 'I couldn't claim to have any friends here,' he said, 'not as we understand the term. Just the odd acquaintance. As for Randall, I know him well enough to exchange a pint if we meet in the pub and happen to feel sociable. But he isn't somebody I'd want to know better than that. There's something sly about him.'

I relaxed. 'Some day,' I said, 'I'll tell you all about it. That I promise. For the moment, I need to know all you can tell me about Randall, but no word must get back to him that I'm interested in him. That's vital.'

'You've got it,' Gordon said simply. 'Now, what can I tell you? What do you want to know?'

'Anything you can tell me.'

He linked his hands behind his head and stared up at the ceiling. 'Bill Randall . . . He's small, thin, dark and ebullient. Volatile might be a better word. Usually cheerful, but he can go down into the dumps or lose his rag over things that you or I would laugh off. And once he's got a bee in his bonnet it never gets out again. High cheekbones and a small mouth – in looks, he reminds me a little of CSM Grant.' Gordon's eyes returned to my level. 'You remember him?'

We wasted a minute or two remembering CSM Grant, who had terrorised the men in his company and worked them unmercifully but would have faced up to a field marshal in defence of any one of them who had got himself into trouble. We got back to Randall at last.

'He runs a farm shop,' Gordon said, 'so he's away from here on most weekdays except that they shut on Thursdays. You know the sort of place?'

'Wellies and oilskins at about a third of the price you'd pay elsewhere?'

'That sort of thing. But he's the local agent for one of the farm-machinery companies. The shop seems to be well run but I don't know that I'd buy a second-hand tractor off him. I don't think that he's short of a few quid. He's never tidy but his wife's always well dressed. She's thin and big-boned; not very attractive, but her heart's in the right place and I'd trust her ten times as far as I'd trust her husband.'

Mention of a wife reminded me. 'Do they smoke?' I asked.

Gordon blinked at me in surprise. 'I never see her without a cigarette in her mouth. He sometimes smokes a small cigar.'

The black cloud which had settled above my head at Dalry began to lift at last. We could be on the right track, but did it go anywhere? Leading questions might reveal too much to Gordon. I trusted his good intentions, but tongues can slip. I tried to think of an oblique approach.

'What interests does he have, outside of the business?' I asked cautiously.

'Not a lot, now, except for the pub.'

I nearly missed it, but the word 'now' caught my ear. 'And earlier?'

'He used to shoot a lot. Wild-fowling, and he had access to several small farms, he and another chap. The farm shop must have given him some useful introductions.'

'He gave up shooting?' I waited anxiously. Something was coming, I knew it.

Gordon reached for a can of beer. He raised his eyebrows at me but I shook my head. He poured with care. 'Say rather that it gave him up. He still goes to the clay pigeons with his pal, to the Cardenden Gun Club – I've heard them talking about it. As I understand it, you can use a borrowed gun quite legally at an approved ground without needing to hold a shotgun certificate.'

'Lost his certificate, did he?'

Gordon nodded. 'He strayed onto Lord Crail's land with a gun. He was fined and the police jerked his certificate.' Gordon paused to take a pull at his beer. 'The way he tells it – and, remember, I've heard only his side of the story – he was shooting near the march. On that farm, he had permission to shoot pheasants. A cock pheasant got up, well out in front of him. He fired at it and was sure that he'd missed. His dog – a nice little spaniel bitch but not very well

97

trained – didn't agree. She took off after it across the boundary.

'When he reached the fence, he could see the dog at the edge of one of Crail's best coverts, running riot among the pheasants. He says that he followed her up as quickly as he could in order to get her back under control and, like an idiot, in his haste he forgot to leave his gun on his own side of the boundary. Just as he caught up with her, she pegged a hen pheasant which had been sitting tight. He took it away from her and the head keeper chose that moment to appear. He – the keeper – hit the roof.'

'That I can believe,' I said. Lord Crail's head keeper was a retired warrant officer from the Scots Guards and he regarded each pheasant as his personal baby and a poacher as something lower than a soldier with a dirty rifle.

'Right,' Gordon said. 'There had already been bad blood, because those pheasants had wandered from Crail's land in the first place. It was quite legal, if opportunist, for Randall to shoot them while they were over the boundary, but it didn't make for good relations. The upshot was that they made a case of it. Crail pushed it for all it was worth. Randall had been shooting alone, so his usual companion wasn't along to back up his version of the story. End of shotgun certificate.'

Lord Crail, a regular client of ours, was the mildest of men but he lived in terror of his head

98

keeper. Crail might have pressed the prosecution but I was ready to bet that the ex-RSM had been pushing Lord Crail. Randall had my qualified sympathy. A spaniel that suddenly runs amok presents the handler with a thousand problems and Crail, whose own dogs were often guilty, knew it as well as I did.

I tiptoed around the question that was at the forefront of my mind. 'Could happen to anybody,' I said. 'Anybody who didn't have the sense to leave his gun on the right side of the fence. It wouldn't make the dog popular.'

'It didn't,' said Gordon. 'That springer had been the apple of his eye. You'd know more about it than I do but, from what the doggy people were saying, I gather that he'd brought her on too quickly in training and had turned a blind eye to certain danger signals. Then he blamed her for the loss of his sport when his own incompetence was to blame. He took a real spite against that poor little bitch. Whenever he got uptight about not being able to go shooting any more, he'd give her another beating. He seemed to think that he could knock the devilment out of her.'

'Instead of which,' I said, 'he should have gone right back to basic training from the beginning. That way, he could have had her rock-steady by the time he got his certificate back.'

'That's what I thought.' Gordon sighed and a shadow passed over his cheerful face. 'I suppose he was just blowing off steam. The Randalls live near the far end of the village but on a calm night we could sometimes hear her . . . But I won't go on about it. The memory makes me feel sick and I haven't been able to stay in the man's company since it began. Somebody made a complaint to the SSPCA but as far as I know they didn't do much about it.'

'You seem to be speaking in the past tense,' I said. 'It's stopped, has it?'

Gordon, who had been leaning back in his chair and talking to the ceiling sat up suddenly and focused on me. 'If it's the springer you're after, she comes of first-class stock but I think you're too late. I haven't seen her around for a few days.'

'You think he's got rid of her?'

'Or had her put down. I'm an early riser and I'm usually settled here before the first shift of dog-walkers – the husbands – goes out. Then, about nine-thirty, when the kids are at school, the breakfast dishes are done and the washing machine's doing its own thing, the second wave begins. That's the wives. Mrs Randall used to come past here with the dog every morning, regular as clockwork. I still see her around but I haven't seen the dog for a while. If you're think-ing of selling Randall a replacement, you'll have to wait until he gets his shotgun certificate back, if he ever does.'

'He should be training another one now,' I

said. 'But I wouldn't sell a spaniel to a man I couldn't trust to treat it well. So. How does Randall occupy his leisure now? Has he taken up stamp collecting? Or photography?'

Again, Gordon looked at me curiously. 'Each time I think I can see a pattern in your questions, you ask something that makes my mind boggle – whatever "boggle" means.' He stretched out for a fat dictionary and leafed through it. 'Did you know that "boggle" comes from the Scots word "bogle"? Meaning ghosties and ghoulies and things that go bump in the night? Never mind. No, as far as I know he doesn't have any hobbies. He wouldn't have the patience and he can get all the photography he needs done for him without bothering himself. His pal's the photographer. Tony Jarrow, the shooting companion.'

'A professional?' I asked.

'He's only an amateur camera buff but he's well equipped and he has his own darkroom. Wins prizes in local competitions sometimes.

'I think Jarrow was relieved rather than otherwise when Randall lost his certificate. He got their shooting to himself and, anyway, their dogs never got on. Jarrow has a boisterous young Labrador which bounced all over poor Duchess – the spaniel. So I don't suppose you'll get to sell many dogs around here.'

'I'm not on a selling trip today,' I said. 'But I'd be interested to know if anybody around here suddenly acquired a new springer bitch.'

Gordon gave me a puzzled look and then shook his head in irritation. 'I'll keep an eye on the dog-walkers and let you know if I spot any new acquisitions. You know, I'd made up my mind that you were being blackmailed but now I'm not so sure. When do I get to know what the hell this is all about?'

His question, which was a natural one, brought me up with a jolt. The neat confluence of information had lulled me into a feeling that our troubles were almost over. I realised suddenly that we had taken only a small step forward and that a solution was still beyond the horizon. Gordon might all too soon see his question answered in the popular press. And, I thought grimly, if any paper referred to me in a headline as 'Dog Man', I would definitely sue.

'I'll come back as soon as I can and spill the beans,' I said. 'You already have my promise. Meantime—'

'More questions?'

'Only one, but in several parts. Then I'll let you get back to your writing.'

He laughed and waved a dismissive hand. 'Don't worry about that. An hour of interesting chat is worth a week of slogging away at the magic machine. I can only do so much original work in a day, a week or a year. After that, even worse rubbish comes out. Between times, I need to listen and talk, get the feel of human contact.

Around here, I only get the bland public face of comparative strangers. Ask away.'

I took a little time to order my thoughts and decide exactly what I did want to know. 'I need to establish a link between either of those men – or their aunts and cousins – and one or more of a different lot living over in my direction. It's a long shot, but you may have seen them together or heard a name mentioned. Start with Aubrey Stoneham. Does the name mean anything?'

'Very little. If it's the same man, I've seen it in the paper when he's opening a fete or pontificating about dogs. I don't know that I've ever set eyes on him.'

'He's tall,' I said, 'and, unless you're titled or in Parliament or the owner of a million acres, the way he looks at you makes you keep glancing down to see whether your flies are open. His face seems to be in Technicolor. Maybe that's because I only see him after a day in the cold air, but I don't think it's that. Broken veins, brown shadows and although he's lost most of his hair his stubble comes in blue and doesn't take much time to do it. A long nose that seems to have been finished in a pencil sharpener. His mouth goes up on the left as though he were smiling. That ought to give him an enigmatic look like the Mona Lisa but it only makes him look crafty. I've never seen him in anything but the sort of clothes that go with a Range Rover, which is what he usually drives.'

103

'If you hadn't said that about his mouth,' Gordon said, 'I'd have told you that I could think of three or four of him. But they all live here in the Neuk of Fife. You paint a good word-picture. If I'd ever seen him, I'd have recognised it.'

'Skip Aubrey Stoneham, then,' I said. I thought about Arthur Lansdyke's other neighbours. 'Try Tony Ellingworth. Also tall. His nose is thin but it's as colourful as Stoneham's. For all I know, the rest of his face would match it, but most of it's hidden behind a beard which is usually long and untidy. When it's trimmed – by his wife using a hedge-trimmer, I think – he can pass for respectable from the neck up. From there down, he's scruffy on principle. When the beard's short, it reveals an Adam's apple that bobs when he talks. He looks as though he buys next year's clothes now and buries them in the garden for the winter. Not much chin inside the beard, which is greying. Hair the same.'

'Don't go on,' Gordon said. 'I know the type. And I'm afraid it's another no.'

'Dan Sievewright, then?' I said. 'Not so tall, more the sturdy type. One of those craggy, heavily modelled faces. He comes close to being every girl's dream of macho but just misses the mark – his mouth seems not to have had enough room to grow between his nose and his chin, as though his teeth had worn down. Imagine something between Omar Sharif and Mr Punch. Brown curly hair. If looks alone counted, the film industry would cast him as a financier or politician who's not on the side of the angels, but he's a farmer and you'd know it – dungarees when working and a stiff suit when he goes to market. Gravelly voice. And a hell of a chip on his shoulder although he doesn't always let you see it.'

Gordon shook his head. 'We're not doing very well,' he said.

'E for effort,' I said. 'Dan's brother's similar, just as macho but with a longer face and straighter hair. Good looking and he knows it. He's the quiet, stay-at-home one but he's a devil with women. Never goes anywhere without his collie bitch. He's moved through to the west coast now.'

'Then need we bother with him? Not that I've ever seen him.'

'He could still have furnished the connection I'm looking for,' I said, 'but if you haven't seen him that's that.' I was about to give up when another name came into my head. 'How about Dougal Henshaw? I've only seen him once and then he was dressed for wild-fowling, so I don't know whether he's as bulky as he looked or if most of it was all the sweaters under his oilskins. But he wouldn't be easy to mistake. Dark hair, ginger eyebrows, a boxer's nose and an upper tooth missing in front. And protruding ears.'

Gordon shook his head again and my spirits fell. Unless one of my suspects had a connection with Randall or Jarrow quite unknown to Gordon, we would have to extend our list. Or, of course, coincidence might have thrown up the wrong two names. Perhaps we were still groping in the dark for an enemy who could see.

'I'm not being much help,' Gordon said. 'In fact, I'm fairly sure that there's only one person, another farmer, whom I've met in Bill Randall's company and who's from your end of the Kingdom.' Gordon was referring to the Kingdom of Fife – an historical legacy not recognised anywhere else in the UK. Gartnaidh and the seven sons of Cruithne may be dead and long forgotten but, to the true Fifer, Fife was never a County and will never be a Region but will remain a Kingdom. Gordon might still feel like an outcast but he was already adopting local habits.

'Who would that be?' I asked.

'I'll have to think. Randall often brings farmers back for a drink at the pub, or a meal if the deal's been big enough – they feed you well without bleeding you dry. I bumped into him once in the bar when he was with one of them and exchanged a drink or two. A stringy man in his fifties with a malicious twist to his mouth. He said that he farmed not far from Cupar.' Gordon closed his eyes. 'Upper something . . .'

I hid my excitement but Gordon must have sensed something. He opened his eyes. 'Have I rung the bell?'

'The answer to that,' I said, 'is a qualified maybe. The description fits my neighbour.'

'Whose name,' Gordon said, 'is Andrew . . . Andrew Williamson. It's come back to me. Am I right?'

'Too right for comfort,' I said.

Some of my appetite had returned and when Gordon asked me to stay for lunch I accepted. He fried steaks and I ate most of mine while we asked, belatedly, after each other's wives and spoke about army days and girls we had known. For a short while we recaptured a little of the camaraderie of service life.


## EIGHT


The sun was behind the hill before I got back to Three Oaks and the afternoon was almost gone.

Henry had again come over to help out and had spent most of the morning changing the combination setting on all the padlocks. The business seemed to have managed very well without me. Two pups had been sold, Ember's service as a stud-dog had been booked for the following week and an owner, on the point of being sent abroad on a short contract, had left a young pointer for advanced training.

I helped to distribute the evening feed, meanwhile repeating the new combination over and over to myself. When the dogs were fed and settled we retired to the house, switched on the microphones and put a match to the logs in the sitting-room fireplace. Work might resume later, but a rehash of the day's events and a discussion of future plans, all over a sociable drink, was our usual milestone for the end of the day's routine.

That evening, we had more to discuss than sheep ticks, competitions and breeding policy. When we were settled with two gin and tonics, one whisky and a can of the stout that Beth always hopes will put some flesh on my bones, I told them in detail of my visit to Gordon Hemmeling.

When I had finished, there was a pause.

'Wow!' Beth said at last. She left the room, leaving the door open.

'I can't quarrel with that comment,' Isobel said. 'We've been lucky. Or I think we have. You're absolutely sure that nothing happened that could make waves?'

'As sure as I can reasonably be,' I said.

Henry polished off half his whisky and put the glass reluctantly aside. 'You're making progress,' he said. 'Let's take it apart and see where you've got to. You seem to have tracked down a brace of men who, between them, were quite capable of supplying the photographs and a spaniel that had obviously been abused.'

'And the man's spaniel hasn't been seen around since before Walnut turned up here,' Isobel said.

'Quite so. I think we can assume that we're on the right track. And John has also established a connection, however tenuous, with Andrew Williamson, the farmer whose land abuts on yours—'

'And who shot a springer spaniel once before for chasing sheep,' Isobel said. 'Not one of ours, only one of those show-bench creatures belonging to that awful woman,' she added, as though that made the deed forgivable. 'What's more, he's had it in for John ever since . . . What was it you said to him?'

I thought back. 'He said that he shot any dog that chased his sheep. And I said that I shot any man who lifted a gun to one of my dogs.'

'Well then!'

Beth had returned and was leafing through the fat working diary in which almost every happening at Three Oaks is recorded, for transferring to accounts or to card index later. 'We've got more than you think,' she said. 'I keep a note of the names of people who come to the Masterclass, mostly in case they leave something behind or go off with some of our equipment. Here it is. A man named Jarrow twice brought a young Labrador, May and June. I remember him, because there weren't many there in June, even considering that it was the slack time of year, and I knew all the others. He took a whole lot of photographs of his own dog but he also photographed John's training methods. I thought of asking him for copies.'

'If we don't get to the bottom of this soon,' I said, 'you may be able to clip them out of the daily paper.'

Isobel held out her glass and I got up to refill it. 'It seems conclusive,' she said. 'Let's accept Randall and Jarrow as accomplices in the frame-up. But I can't buy all of it. I can visualise Andrew Williamson as a spiteful back-stabber. Assume that he shot a spaniel as he did once before. He might have thought that it was one of ours. He wouldn't believe for a moment that John would really shoot him in revenge, but he might expect some sort of retaliation. So he might get his friends to cook up something to keep us quiet. But he's – what? – more than six miles from Kilcolm.'

'More like seven,' I said.

'Not across country, the way a dog would come,' Beth said shyly. 'Perhaps four and a half or five.'

Isobel was not used to being set right by Beth, who was half her age but looked a third of it. It took her a second or two to get going again. 'Even so,' she said firmly. 'I've known a dog wander that far, if he's been walked in that direction and knows that there's a bitch there. In fact, he might have been making for here. Next time that Mr Lansdyke phones, whoever takes the call must ask him whether Horace was

110

walked near here during the few days before he was shot. He might have got a whiff of Stardust's false season.'

'You're making a good case against Williamson,' I said. 'What is it that you can't believe?'

'This,' Isobel said firmly. 'Could you see Horace making his way five miles home again after being shot as severely as he was?'

I had to admit that it seemed unlikely. 'But you never know,' I said. 'If he was desperate enough and before his wounds stiffened up . . .'

'Andrew Williamson might have read the address on Horace's collar,' Beth said. 'He could have taken him as far as the gate of Kilcolm by car and pushed him out.'

'Horace wasn't wearing a collar when he was brought here,' Isobel said. 'All right, so Mr Lansdyke might have taken it off to make him more comfortable. In that case, what would have triggered the particular piece of spite against us?'

Beth was struggling. 'Somebody else might have found Horace and driven him home. Mr Williamson could still think that he'd shot one of our dogs.'

'Then why didn't your "someone else" drive up to the door of Kilcolm?' Isobel demanded. 'And we don't know of any connection between Williamson and Aubrey Stoneham. Stoneham isn't his landlord, is he?'

'The farm belongs to Lord Crail,' I told her.

'That doesn't mean that no connection exists,'

Henry said. 'The connection may be between Stoneham and Jarrow or Randall. But just how we check on that I'm damned if I know.'

'We could ask Charles Buccleugh to do some telephoning,' I said. 'He must know everybody who dislikes Stoneham. If there's a connection, one of them would know it. But I think it's too much of a risk.'

'Definitely,' Beth said.

Henry and Isobel were looking at me hopefully. I got up and refilled their glasses. I usually put our drinks bill to the tax-man as 'entertaining overseas clients'. It was a drain on our profit, but if our profit was intended to buy booze anyway . . .

'If it's only spite,' Isobel said, 'a complaint would have been made by now. Well, where do we go from here?'

There was another uncomfortable silence.

'What about Stardust?' Beth asked suddenly. 'Somebody must be keeping her. One of the three.'

'A lot more than three,' I said.

'If she's alive,' Isobel said, 'which I wouldn't bet on, she could be being kept by anybody anywhere. It's easy enough to board a dog out. If any one of us goes poking around looking for a missing dog, the fat could really be in the fire.'

Silence fell again.

'We've made enough progress for one day,'

Henry said at last. 'I think we should sleep on it.'

His advice was too sensible and too negative to be immediately accepted, but after an age of fruitless discussion we agreed to do just that.

I helped Beth to wash up after a belated evening meal and was first into bed. Beth spent an age downstairs and when she came up she was in pensive mood. She pottered around, undressing in easy stages, spent more time in the bathroom than I would have believed possible and finally made it into a short nightgown. Then, arms raised and hair-brush in hand, she paused.

'Suppose Mr Stoneham was trying to mislead us,' she said. 'Perhaps the questions you'd been asking about Horace were only an excuse for putting the screws on us.'

'Out of spite?'

'Maybe, maybe not. There could be something we don't know about yet.'

'Like what?' I asked.

'I don't know like what. If I could think of it, I'd have said.'

'Hurry up and come to bed before you freeze.' I said it reluctantly. Beth, in her prettiest nightie and with hair-brush still poised, looked like something off one of the glamour calendars which I secretly admire.

She finished brushing her hair and got into

bed, putting cold feet on my legs. 'Warm me up,' she said.

I put an arm around her. 'I suppose it's possible,' I said.

'What is?'

'What you were suggesting. If somebody wanted us out of business. But I can't see any reason. There's enough competition in this business that our removal from it wouldn't leave anybody a clear field. No, either it's to stop us looking into Horace or it's spite.'

'Or somebody wanted to get their hands on Stardust. Or get rid of Walnut. Or something. You've trodden on enough toes from time to time. Perhaps he's helping a friend to get his own back.' She sighed deeply. The sigh moved her soft body against me.

The incessant talk about a threat to our livelihood and the impossibility of arriving at any logical conclusions from the facts available had dominated my thinking for too long. Now I only wished to clear my mind and try to sleep. Beth seemed to sense my renewed depression.

She clasped her arms around my waist and squeezed until I was almost out of breath. 'You're not to worry about it,' she said. 'We'll still be happy and in business ten years from now. I promise you. Have you ever known me make a promise I couldn't keep?'

I wanted to believe her. We hugged each other in the darkness and in exchanging reassurance we felt a renewal of passion. My sex-life had been spasmodic and uncertain since my illness; but the search for balm, to take and to give, brought a special poignancy to the act.

For once, neither of us had cause to be disappointed. In retrospect, it seems certain that our child was conceived that night.

I was up and about in good time. Beth, usually the earliest of risers but languorous that morning, watched me from under her tumbled hair and I knew that she was wondering whether my old insomnia was back. I was able to assure her that my unusual energy was accounted for by a better sleep than I had had in many days.

The early morning garden smelled deliciously of frosted greenery. I went first to sit in the run of the isolation kennel. I tried the newcomer with the name Duchess, but the name had bad vibes for her and she responded better to Walnut. I had to start with her again, if not from Square One then from Square Two or Three, and earn her trust afresh, but the process was quicker and easier.

Beth came out of the house and threw herself into the basic chores of feeding, grooming, cleaning out and exercising. My new pupil, the pointer, had settled in well. I put him through an elementary test to be sure that his early training had not been skipped, but once he had accepted me he passed with flying colours. I went on to give the older dogs a workout, one at a time, with dummies on the lawn, coaxing the timid, steadying the headstrong and trying always to anticipate the faults towards which each dog might become prone.

Isobel, who had walked over as usual, decided to spend some time with Horace – who still failed to respond – and then to look over the stores in her tiny surgery. Each of us wore a thoughtful frown but, by common agreement, we put off discussion until we had done our thinking.

I was preparing to take one or two of our more advanced competitors further afield for some exercise with the gun when Isobel came out of the house.

'How's the patient?' I asked.

'Horace? Still frightened for himself. I wanted to try a little massage, to get some movement going again, but he thinks I'm going to pull his leg off.' She produced a sheet of paper. 'I have a list here . . .'

The list was of items which she insisted must be replaced immediately so that she could be prepared for an outbreak of this or that. She could have borrowed my car, or walked home to take Henry's, but there was a long-standing conspiracy to keep her out from behind the wheel whenever possible. Not only was she temperamentally unsuited to driving and so was a general danger on the roads, but if she happened to meet a convivial friend while she was in a vulnerable mood our usually reliable partner was quite capable of getting herself locked up and disqualified.

Beth had deserted the puppies for the moment. She made faces at me from behind Isobel's back until I volunteered to double up a trip to Easter Colm with a couple of dogs and doing Isobel's shopping along the way.

I drove first to Cupar. The streets, as usual, were busy. The hub of Cupar is a T-junction where a broad street leads south towards Kirkcaldy from the main road to St Andrews. I tried that area and managed to slot the car into one of the end-on spaces, almost outside Woolworth's, saving myself a walk from a peripheral carpark.

Isobel's list contained nothing exclusively veterinary. Returning with her purchases from Boots, I was unlocking the car door when a police car coasted to a halt across its tail and PC Peel, the constable who had sought my help over the fox, got out of the driver's seat. He gave me a friendly grin and obviously expected one in return.

The last thing that I wanted was to be seen talking to any policeman. It might have been my visit to Kilcolm in his company that had provoked the frame-up in the first place. The usual stream of vehicles was crawling along the main road a stone's throw away and, although there was not enough traffic where we were to encourage him to move on, the pavements were busy. I could have pleaded that I was in a hurry, but in my experience that ploy only necessitates more time-wasting explanations. Short of telling him to get out of the way or be rammed, I was stuck.

'Good morning to you,' he said.

I put my purchases down and returned the greeting.

'Seeing you there, I thought I'd just stop and tell you that we found the man who left the fox in the tree. Somebody spotted another snare and saw a man heading in that direction and I was in time to catch him visiting his snare. He's been warned about his future behaviour.'

I had intended to keep my mouth shut. If somebody saw me listening in silence to a homily from the constable, I could hardly be blamed. But curiosity overcame me. 'Who was it?' I asked.

'I'd be out of order to tell you that.'

'Not Tony Ellingworth?' I was remembering the Ellingworth chickens.

Constable Peel chuckled and leaned his elbows on the roof of my car. I realised that I should have kept to my resolution. This would be good for another five minutes. 'Not him,' he said. 'He couldn't set a snare to save his life. I know him quite well. Did you know that he's moving away soon?'

I was still consumed with impatience. Also I was getting cold and I wanted a pee. But the

118

constable's gossip was becoming ever more interesting. 'No, I didn't,' I said.

'I spotted him an hour ago, coming out of the dogfood shop.' Peel nodded across the road. 'I stopped to ask him if he'd be at the clay pigeons on Thursday.'

'We can't be talking about the same Ellingworth,' I said. 'The one I know doesn't have a gun of his own.'

Peel was chatting comfortably but his eyes were missing no detail of the passing traffic. 'No more does this one. He and Dan Sievewright of Easter Colm usually go through to the mart at Dunfermline together on Thursdays and they stop off at the Cardenden Gun Club on the way back. I'm a member and I'm usually there on a Thursday if I'm off duty. Mr Ellingworth borrows Mr Sievewright's gun. It doesn't fit him well but he gets by. He could be good if his heart was in it and he got his own gun.'

That explained the puzzle of why Tony Ellingworth had a shotgun certificate but no gun of his own. On an unapproved ground he would need a certificate even to use a borrowed gun. But if the constable's words answered one question they raised at least one other.

'I didn't think those two liked each other much,' I said.

'They get on all right, when they're on the loose. Boys together out of school. The only friction between them was that Mr Sievewright always wanted to get his hands on Ellingworth's bit of land – and his house. Easter Colm farmhouse is only fit for demolition. Sometimes they'd needle each other about it in the clubhouse. Ellingworth was holding out, but now he's agreed to sell his place to Mr Sievewright and he's heading off down south again.' The radio in his car began to chatter. 'Time I wasn't here,' Peel said. 'Just thought I'd give you the news.'

He got back into the car and drove off. I went and relieved myself in the Drookit Dug and then sat in the car for a few minutes before following. So there was a connection between both Sievewright and Ellingworth, through the Cardenden Gun Club, to Randall and Jarrow. And Thursday, which was the day of the Dunfermline mart, was also the day the farm shop closed.

Well, well, well!

I drove past Kilcolm to Easter Colm, giving less thought to the Highway Code than to any possible consequences of my accidental encounter. It might not matter if I had been seen in deep discussion with Constable Peel in Cupar. There were plenty of innocuous topics which could have been engrossing us, although I wished that I had thought to brandish my driving licence aloft while we spoke. Best, I thought, to carry on as normal. Any change to my routine might be taken by our invisible enemy to signal a threat.

There was unlikely to be much but rabbits on Easter Colm, but rabbits can provide the basis of good training provided that the dog is under tight control, and myxomatosis had thinned them to vanishing point nearer home. I parked beside a barn and took Lucy and my gun out of the car. I had noticed the dilapidated state of the house earlier but now, looking at it in the light of Constable Peel's remarks, I could see that there was a sag to the roof and that one gable was leaning.

Lucy knew that sport was coming and she wanted to dance, but discipline held and she sat, shuffling gradually forward on her bottom, while I strapped on a cartridge belt and added a coat against a day which was turning bitterly cold. She stayed tight at heel until I cast her out and then she fell into a quartering pattern in front of me, well within gunshot.

A tractor was working in the distance, ploughing over what had been the rough set-aside land behind the Old Manse. That was where many of the rabbits had dwelt. I felt sad. Another useful wild-life haven was being sacrificed on the altar of prairie farming. I headed in that direction, putting Lucy through the hedge-bottoms along the way; but the few rabbits broke out on the other side of the hedge and we arrived at the ploughing without getting the chance of a shot.

Dan Sievewright, at the wheel of the tractor, had only a few more passes to make. He gave me a nod as he went by. Some of the rabbits would already have fled or have been buried in their burrows, but my guess was that a few would have been driven into the remaining strip of long grass and weeds and would bolt at the last moment. I took up a position, looking along the field of dark plough towards the hedge bordering the Old Manse Garden.

There was no sign of any of the Ellingworths although what I could see of the garden looked tidier than usual. The bonfire had been rebuilt on its previous site and was sending a column of smoke through the leafless branches. The small fields belonging to the Old Manse, which Ellingworth had kept for grazing his few sheep or renting to pony riders, would certainly let Dan Sievewright improve his ploughing pattern by turning two large L-shaped fields into tidy rectangles.

The tractor began its last cut. Lucy looked past me suddenly and I swung round, too late, as a rabbit broke out behind me and bobbed away towards the nearest ditch. I could see the tips of the grasses moving as rabbits darted ahead of the plough. Then they broke all at once, a dozen or more, streaming out and heading across the grass for the ditch or the hedge beyond. I bowled two over, reloaded and caught another before it was out of range. The nearest was still kicking.

Lucy had held steady. She wanted to go for the one that was kicking on the bare earth a few yards from us but I sent her for the furthest and picked up the two nearer ones myself, as a reminder that she was not there to do anything but what she was told to do. She returned with the rabbit hanging limp in her jaws as I finished the *coup de grâce*, and she delivered it to hand, sitting.

While I hung the rabbits in the leather loops of my game carrier, Dan Sievewright had halted the tractor at the end of his last furrow and stopped the engine. He jumped down and lit a cigarette before leaning back against the muddy wheel. He was looking at me. Evidently I was expected to walk to him.

He was in an uncharacteristically friendly mood. 'Yon wee dog's good,' he said as I came up.

'She's coming along,' I said. 'She's had a win in an open stake already.'

'What'll you be asking for her?'

I told him and he gave a scandalised whistle. 'We couldn't sell her for less,' I said. 'Not if we add up my time and all the food she's eaten, plus a dozen other oncosts. If you can buy Tony Ellingworth's place, you can surely afford the price of a first-class shooting dog.'

'Who told you that I was buying the Old Manse?' he asked sharply, defensive as always.

It was my chance to start broadcasting the true version of my activities. 'One of the local bobbies stopped me in Cupar,' I said. 'I'd helped him by explaining a skinned fox that had been left hanging in a tree by Kilcolm and he wanted to tell me the outcome. He'd just had the news from Tony Ellingworth, so he passed it along.'

The conversation seemed to die the death. We both waited. To break the silence, I said, 'I thought this was your set-aside land.'

He scowled, not at me but at some thought. 'It was,' he said. 'George was aye for taking the EEC's money. I told him and told him that it was a bad bargain and no more than making a home for a' the vermin in the world, but he was benset on't. And now look what was adae.'

'What?'

'The dug flourish got intil't, that's what.'

I had heard the Scots expression before but it took me a second or two to pin down. 'Ragwort?' I said.

'Aye. A notifiable weed. The council served a notice on me. A fortune in selective weedkiller. Well, I'm having no more to do wi' their set-asides.'

Rather than start debating the merits and demerits of cereal mountains, wild-life conservation and the European Community, I decided to change the subject. 'George is definitely staying on in the west, then?'

He nodded slowly. 'Found a good wee place near Tarbet,' he said. 'Hill country, but George aye liked working with sheep. We've struck a deal.'

'I dare say you'll both be happier now.'

His eyes were suddenly locked with mine and I disliked the look in them. 'What do you mean by that?' he demanded.

'Nothing in particular,' I said. 'Just that sharing the farm didn't seem to be a comfortable arrangement for either of you.'

He relaxed once more against the tractor's wheel and fumbled out another cigarette. 'It's as bad as sharing a woman,' he said. The idea seemed to amuse him. 'There's more rabbits over by the western march. I mustn't keep you.'

This was a barely polite formula for telling me to go away. I took Lucy back to the car and collected the pointer.

Over lunch, which was the usual snack taken amid a welter of discussion, paperwork, sudden disappearances to attend to remembered tasks and subsequent reheating of resumed meals in the microwave oven, I gave Isobel her packages and told the story of my morning.

Beth tried very hard not to panic when I recounted my kerbside chat with Constable Peel. 'Even if you were seen,' she said, 'surely anybody with any sense would know that you wouldn't be asking questions about shot dogs and faked photographs in a public street, not after being threatened like that. I mean, you just wouldn't.'

'Do you really believe that?' I asked her.

'Believe which? That you wouldn't do it? Or that they wouldn't believe it?'

'The latter,' I said.

She pondered with wrinkled brow for a moment, working out which was the latter. 'I want to believe it. Anyway, you seem to have put Dan Sievewright straight.'

'If he's the one or if he passes it on. And if he believed me.'

Isobel was eating a toasted-cheese sandwich while checking over the contents of her packages. She looked up. 'It could be assumed that you were making a gesture of defiance,' she said with her mouth full. She saw the anxiety in Beth's face and hurried to change the subject. 'I hope you didn't bring back any seeds of ragwort on your clothes. Pernicious stuff!' she added, spraying crumbs.

'I rather hope I did,' I said. 'It's quite easy to deal with in a garden, but it wouldn't move me to tears if Andrew Williamson found it coming up among his cereals – especially if it turns out that he's behind all this harassment.'

'Do you think he is?' Beth asked me. She got up and began to wash dishes.

'I'm damned if I know,' I said. 'His only quarrel with us is that Crail, who's his landlord and holds the sporting rights, gave us permission to shoot over the farm as part of our dog-training and Williamson doesn't make a penny off it. It isn't a permission I've taken advantage of very often, because there's damn-all on the ground. And none of our dogs has ever wandered; but God knows how much it rankled. I think I could believe it of him more easily than of any of the others we've come across. He's the only one who's been openly spiteful.'

'He's a grouchy old wretch,' Isobel said absently, 'but I doubt if he gives a genuine damn. He just enjoys the excuse for a good row with a neighbour.'

'He might also enjoy making a neighbour squirm,' I said. 'Whether or not he shot Horace, if he suddenly found himself in a position to drop us in the clag he might be tempted. He has that malicious sort of humour.'

'Do you think that Stardust might be in his outbuildings somewhere?' Beth asked. 'No, don't answer that. I don't want to be told again that she's probably dead. She had . . . has the sweetest nature of any of our dogs.' Beth had her back to me but I could hear the misery in her voice.

I got up quickly and put an arm around her. 'Not when there's a stud-dog around.'

When she turned, her cheeks were wet with tears. 'It's her privilege to be choosy. If she's alive, I hope they're being kind to her. And if . . . not . . . I hope it was done without fear or pain and I hope we can find them and make them suffer and suffer for it.' I felt a sob shake her body but after a moment she said more

127

calmly, 'Do you really suppose that anybody who's involved saw you this morning and jumped to the wrong conclusion?'

'You keep asking me what I think,' I said, 'and I don't know what to think. We're playing Pin the Tail on nobody in particular, blindfold and in the dark. We'll just have to wait and see.'

We did not have to wait long. The phone rang in the late afternoon while we were preparing the daily feed. I was nearest to the kitchen extension so I answered it.

The voice on the other end was distorted by an echo, as though somebody were speaking through a large tin can which had been opened at both ends, but there was no mistaking the anger and viciousness in the tone nor the meaning in the words. 'You were warned,' it said, 'but you wouldn't take a telling. Now you're going to catch it. You may as well pack up and leave now. You'll be out of business in a month anyway.'

The caller hung up before I could say a word.

I slumped into one of the fireside chairs before my knees could let me down. I must have looked shattered. Beth was staring at me, wide-eyed, and Isobel, who had just come in from one of her regular inspections of our stock for sheep ticks and other infestations, crossed the kitchen quickly and stooped to look into my face.

Isobel sometimes examines me as though I were a sick puppy. 'Are you going to feel my nose?' I asked her. 'Or shove a thermometer up my backside?'

'Sorry,' she said, straightening up. 'For a moment I thought you were going to black out again. What's wrong?'

'That was an anonymous caller,' I said. 'A man's voice, but distorted. He said that we'd been warned and now we were going to catch it.'

Beth spilled puppy meal all over the floor but Isobel kept her head. 'You couldn't recognise the voice? No, you wouldn't if it was distorted. But did he have a strong accent?'

'I thought not,' I said. 'Once I caught on to what he was saying, I listened. He may have been hiding his accent – "talking pan loaf", as they say. His last word was certainly "anyway", not "onywie". But he said "take a telling", which isn't exactly Queen's English.'

'Well, whoever he is, he's off his rocker or crazy with spite,' Isobel said. 'Once he's fired his salvo, his weapon's gone. What do you plan to do?'

I shook my head. My mind had gone blank.

Beth gave up trying to clean up the mess of meal. 'I know what I plan to do,' she said shakily. 'And that's to get our story in first. Whoever they make a stink with, the SSPCA will be consulted and I don't want us to be caught on the defensive.' She leaned past me and plucked the phone off the wall. 'What's Mr Hautry's number?'

I looked up the number for her. She dialled. Alex Hautry, it seemed, was in his office.

'Oh, Mr Hautry,' Beth said. 'It's Mrs Cunningham at Three Oaks . . . We're fit and well, thank you, but we have a problem and we need to see you . . . Yes, it is urgent but' – she looked at the window – 'but I think we need daylight. Could you pay us a visit tomorrow morning? And, please, whatever comes to your attention concerning us before then, do nothing until we've spoken to you. We think that false allegations are being made against us . . . You promise? Bless you, that's a relief! Oh, and be sure to wear your kilt. I'll explain when I see you . . . Tomorrow, then.' For some seconds she listened to what was, to me, only a faint quacking from the receiver. 'I quite understand. Goodbye.'

She hung up the phone and looked from one to the other of us. 'How did I do?'

'Admirably,' Isobel said. 'How did he respond?'

Beth's young face seemed to have aged with anxiety. 'He said that he wouldn't go off at half-cock, but I could tell that he has his reservations. If he decides that we're guilty . . .'

'He mustn't,' I said.

'No, he mustn't. But I think he feels he was stupid over that fox. He was trying to explain to me that he'd never seen a skinned fox before.'

'I saved him from making an idiot of himself,' I pointed out.

'He may not see it that way. People aren't always grateful for that sort of thing. You go and put your kilt on. Don't look at me as though one of us is dottled,' she said. 'Isobel and I can manage to feed the dogs without your help. I'm going to bring Walnut indoors and you can spend your time fraternising with her. By the time Mr Hautry comes we want her—'

'Eating out of my hand?' I suggested.

Beth made an impatient gesture. 'She already does that. We want to be able to show him that she dotes on you. Just don't let her get up on the furniture,' she added sternly.


## NINE


When Beth came to us first as our kennel-maid and general dogsbody, she was in quite irrational awe of me – intimidated, perhaps, by the cruel edge that my tongue develops when illness has brought me low. But from the moment when she first saw my feet of clay, she developed an attitude as protective as that of a Doberman bitch over her litter. It is no use my protesting that I am very much better than I was; as long as the local quack shakes his head and tuts over me, as he does over every patient, Beth continues to protect me from stress, physical or mental. On almost every other subject she is deferential, sometimes excessively so when I am in need of advice or at least a joint decision; but when she thinks my health is at risk she becomes mother and nanny and wardress rolled into one intimidating package.

In the morning, that mood was on her and I knew that resistance would only strengthen it. To tell the truth, I was a little below par after a night during which bad dreams had alternated with sleepless worrying and I was happy to be fed and settled in a chair in the sitting-room in front of a log fire with some of the endless paperwork, usually attended to by Isobel, to keep me occupied while Isobel took over my training duties.

Gentle persuasion was going to be the order of the day when Hautry arrived and Beth was far better than I was at wheedling. She did the chores in her habitual jeans and sweater, but as soon as they were finished she changed into one of her prettier dresses and I noticed that she had taken more trouble than usual over her hair and makeup. The man from the SSPCA was going to be wheedled as he had never been wheedled before.

I heard Alex Hautry's car arrive but, as ordered, I stayed put, checking through our account books to see who still owed us money. The total turned out to be less than I had hoped. It was an hour later and I was trying to make sense of our VAT returns before I heard voices in the hall. I stacked my papers and got up to dump them thankfully on a side table for Isobel's attention and shake hands.

Hautry was a man in his thirties with red hair and a thin face. His smooth skin made him look almost girlish until one noticed the square jaw and a strong mouth. He was kilted and I saw that he was carrying the photograph. He shook my hand guardedly and accepted a chair. Beth perched on the arm of mine.

Isobel followed them into the room a few seconds later, accompanied by Walnut. The spaniel bitch was nervous. She looked round at the several figures. For a moment, it looked as though she would bolt for her life. Then, deciding that she recognised a friend, she came over and put her paws on my knee to nose my sporran. I gave her a biscuit and she settled on the hearthrug. I saw Hautry's eyes follow her and felt Beth sigh with relief.

'Yes,' Hautry said. 'Well. Your wife's told me the whole unlikely story and I've made the acquaintance of the dog you call Walnut.'

'And?' I said.

'It's early days to be sure.' Caught between an overdose of Beth at her most persuasive and an habitual suspicion of most animal owners, Hautry was trying hard to be impartial. And I guessed that the incident of the fox had caused him some loss of face and it still rankled.

Beth stiffened. 'She wouldn't have come to

John like that if he'd been in the habit of beating her.'

'You never know, with dogs. She has certainly been abused, but the leader of the pack remains the leader, whatever. I've seen cases in which a dog which had been starved and beaten over a long period still fawned over its master. But,' he said firmly before Beth could protest again, 'I've studied the photograph and visited the scene. The photograph isn't sharp and the trunk of one oak can look very like another, but, try as I may, I can't find a viewpoint in which the outline of the tree and the skyline beyond both agree with the photograph. Mrs Cunningham assures me that there's no other oak near by.'

'There isn't,' I said.

'That's not conclusive. Of course, if the other photograph comes into my hands – the one that Mrs Cunningham says is genuine but innocuous – and if it was clearly taken here, that would go some way towards confirming your story. Also, I think that this' – he flicked the photograph, which was becoming tatty and dog-eared with much handling – 'was taken in autumn or winter. I don't know why it gives me that impression, except that it has been focused short and it seems to show dead leaves on the grass.'

'The genuine photograph showed the tree in full leaf,' Beth said.

'I may have the chance to see for myself. But

it could be that the best evidence in your favour will be furnished by the dog herself.'

'Her behaviour?' Beth said.

He shook his head impatiently. 'Her hide. I've examined her with Mrs Kitts and there's a difference in tone between some parts of her coat and others. The signs are very faint, but I'm inclined to agree with Mrs Kitts that it looks as though some of her markings have been extended, using a dye – which has also stained her skin. I've taken some clippings for examination. More to the point, as the hair grows back where I've clipped it, it may come in white at the roots. *If* Mrs Kitts is correct,' he added firmly.

'But we may not be able to wait that long,' Beth said. 'I've shown you photographs of the real Stardust.'

'Not particularly good photographs and without any of the movement that gives a dog character. The visible differences are less than the difference a good brushing would make,' Hautry said. 'I'm sorry. And – please forgive me, Mrs Cunningham, but I have to look at the evidence without bias – I have only your word for it that your photographs are of the missing dog. I appreciate your problem. But, if I'm asked, the most I could say at the moment is that I don't consider the evidence conclusive. And that's assuming that no more conclusive evidence is offered along with any accusation that may be made.'

There was a glum silence which I felt I had to break. 'That's better than nothing,' I said. 'I'm glad we asked you to come over. At least now, if there's a sudden accusation, you'll take a very hard look at any evidence.'

He drew himself up indignantly – not an easy posture to adopt while sitting. 'We always do. On the other hand, if the accusation is made directly to us, that will suggest that it's valid.'

'Why on earth?' Isobel demanded.

'Because our inquiries are as confidential as we can reasonably make them. If, as you suggest, somebody is out to ruin you, he wouldn't go to the police or to us. On the evidence so far, a prosecution would be very unlikely to succeed. No, he'd go straight to the gutter press. Then you would really have a problem. Anything about cruelty to animals is hot news at the moment. So is anything that shows shooting in a discreditable light. And when the tabloids think they're on to a story they blandly ignore any denials or contrary evidence. And there might not be a lot you could do about it. Muck tends to stick.'

He looked around our faces. He was only confirming what we had already told each other, but Beth, for one, was near to tears. 'I didn't want to distress you,' Hautry said, 'but it's better that you think about it now.'

'We haven't thought about much else for days. What would you advise?' I asked him.

He looked at me consideringly for a few

seconds and then he shrugged. 'It's hardly my place to advise you,' he said. 'You may not have much time, but if I were in the position you tell me you're in, I'd consider striking first. If, for instance, you could name the man who had the dog and give me proof that he did the beating . . . Well, consider the effect of a prior charge against somebody else. Do you have a name to give me?'

I looked at Isobel and Beth and could read the same thought in both their faces. We had no more now than the SSPCA had had when they had decided that there was not enough evidence to proceed against William Randall. I shook my head.

'I suggest that you try to get one. If you do, call me again. I may be able to help.'

'He doesn't have the dog any more,' I said. 'He's offloaded her onto us. How on earth could we offer proof?'

'When you know all the facts, proof usually follows.' He nodded in satisfaction, evidently feeling that he had offered us the solution to all our problems. He took one last look at Walnut and made his departure.

Just when we had most need of time to think and discuss, the business hit one of its most demanding streaks. An American, who had purchased a trained dog during the summer, now wanted him sent over by air, immediately if not sooner. Another owner, who had flagrantly ignored all the advice that I had given him at the time of purchase, arrived on the doorstep, insisting that the dog's faults must be hereditary and demanding his money back. A young couple turned up in search of a puppy; Beth mistook them for reporters and nearly drove them off the premises.

Beth then went to the aid of Isobel and a bitch that was whelping early. I divided my time between telephoning the transport agents, assuring the aggrieved purchaser that he had more chance of coming to the throne than of getting his money back and then, despite my own urgent need to bite somebody's head off, administering soothing words to the ruffled young couple. They chose my favourite from among the youngest generation; and they seemed to be taking in my words of counsel, although only time would tell. After endless consultation and mind-changing they left at last, taking with them a dog bed, feeding bowl, lead, collar, the full spectrum of training aids and a supply of dogfood sufficient to see the puppy into adolescence, and leaving behind a most satisfactory cheque. We could have done with more such clients, but preferably some other day.

Henry, summoned by Isobel, had walked over to join us, but any discussion that we managed before late afternoon was fragmentary – and was then made superfluous by a phone-call that came just as we were settling around the kitchen table to thrash things out over a belated afternoon tea.

Beth took the call. She switched on the cheap little amplifier that is permanently attached to the kitchen phone so that the partners can hear both sides of any discussion. As soon as I heard the name of one of the most blatant of the Sunday tabloids, I jumped up and reached for the phone.

Beth pushed me into one of the basket chairs, anchored me firmly by sitting down on my lap and held onto the phone with a vice-like grip. 'We do know about those photographs,' she said clearly. 'They are fakes and we can prove it.'

'We'll quote you on that,' the distant voice said.

'You'd better.' I had never realised that Beth's voice, usually as soft as a spaniel's mouth, could become so hard. 'If you use the story at all.'

'And that's your only comment?'

'Not by a mile. Where are you speaking from?'

'Edinburgh,' said the voice.

'If you publish without sending somebody here to establish the facts,' Beth said, 'we will sue. And, what's more, we'll get very substantial damages. And I have three witnesses to this conversation.'

'Have you finished?'

Beth ignored the question. 'On the other hand, if you have a reporter and a photographer here tomorrow morning with copies of all the photographs, we'll not only give you proof. We can also give you a much bigger and better story.'

I saw Henry and Isobel exchange an agonised glance. I nearly grabbed again for the phone, but Beth had already committed us.

'Exclusive?' The voice sounded more interested.

'Absolutely.'

'Very well,' said the distant voice. 'They'll be there. But if this is no more than a delaying tactic, it won't achieve anything. We can still meet our deadline.' His tone of voice would have suited a judge passing sentence on a child-abuser. Evidently we had already been judged and found guilty.

'That's good,' Beth said firmly. She got off my knee, hung up the phone and looked around defiantly into a shocked silence. 'Well?'

'You haven't left us much room for discussion,' Henry said.

'Because there isn't any. What else could I say? "Publish and be damned"? How else could I have bought us any time at all?' Beth was scared but defiant.

'You couldn't,' Isobel said. 'Only two things will stop a paper publishing – a writ or the promise of a bigger story. But, Beth. What tale are you going to spin them tomorrow?' Isobel, usually the staunchest of the three of us, sounded almost plaintive.

'I don't know yet,' Beth said slowly. 'I'm

beginning to get ideas but I need time to think them through. Give me a hand with the dogs' feed,' she said more briskly. It seemed that there were still only two fixed points in the universe – death and the dogs' dinners. 'Then you two may as well go home. I want John to repeat every word anybody's said to him since this started and everything he's seen and done. There's something in there, only I haven't got it sorted out yet. There has to be.'

'God!' Isobel said. 'I hope so!'

'We could stay,' said Henry. 'We might be able to help.'

Beth shook her head violently. 'Just this once, leave it to me. You'd only muddle me with questions.'

We prepared and delivered the feeds together. Beth was withdrawn and silent. We had seen this mood before. Usually, just when she seemed to have lost her marbles, she turned out to have out-thought the rest of us. I hoped that this was one of the times. If not, our comfortable little business was doomed.

When all was tidied away for the night, Henry and Isobel prepared to go. Isobel caught me out of earshot of Beth. 'She'll have to have something for those reporters in the morning,' she said. 'Does she have something in mind? Or was she bluffing?'

'Beats me,' I said. 'Maybe Beth herself doesn't know yet. If we start throwing accusations

141

around, we'll find ourselves defending a libel action as well as starting another one, on top of our other worries.'

'That's what I thought. Just in case Beth doesn't come up with something, I'm going to go home and have a damned good think, with Henry's help. You'd better do much the same. Somebody's got to have something to say by morning.'

'Believe me, I will.'

'If anything occurs to you, give me a ring.' She looked anxiously into my eyes before turning away.

The door had hardly closed behind them before Beth picked up the phone and dialled a number. I pointed to the amplifier and she turned it on. Charles Buccleugh's voice came on the line.

'It's all coming to a head,' Beth told him. 'We had a threat over the phone and now one of the Sunday papers is sending a reporter to see us tomorrow. We've got to come up with the best answer we can find in a hurry. I wondered whether you'd picked up any more news.'

'Not a thing. And, believe me, I've tried. How did you get on over William Randall?'

'We're sure that he did it, him and a friend,' Beth said. 'But there's no evidence as to who's behind it.'

'I'm sorry,' Buccleugh said. 'I've nothing more to contribute.'

'You might have. When you came over here, you said that your daughter was looking after Tony Ellingworth's children. Is Mrs Ellingworth ill?'

'Not that I know of.' There was a pause on the line. 'I believe that she's left her husband.'

News of marital rifts always interested Beth. 'How long ago?' she asked.

'That I don't know. Young Tony started dumping his brats on us the morning after the big thunderstorm, almost a fortnight ago now. He's been trying to keep it quiet but tongues are wagging.' I heard him sigh. 'Can't say that I blame her. Nice woman and she didn't have a life of it. But I shouldn't be gossiping like this.'

'Yes you should,' Beth said. 'This is the time for gossip. We've nothing to lose now. Would you phone your friends? We want to know of a connection between Mr Randall, or his friend Tony Jarrow, and our neighbour Mr Williamson, the farmer.'

'I'll try,' Buccleugh said. 'I'll call you back if I have any luck. I'm sorry to be such a broken reed on the other thing.'

'You're not a broken reed at all,' Beth said. 'You put us on to Mr Randall. That may turn out to give us exactly the link we need. When this is over, you must come again and spend the day with us and let us pick your brains about something easier, like raising spaniels.'

'I'd enjoy that,' Buccleugh said. 'What brains I have are yours for the picking.'

Beth hung up. The phone rang again immediately. This time, it was Hautry from the SSPCA to say that the newspaper had contacted him for a quote. 'I told him that I had some knowledge of the allegations,' Hautry said, 'and that the evidence I'd seen so far was open to other interpretations. I also said that I'd know more within the week, if they cared to wait for the lab report on the hair samples.'

'They won't, of course,' Beth said.

'No. They'd prefer to print their story while they've still got it, rather than wait for it to be disproved. I'm sorry. I thought that I should let you know.'

Beth thanked him and hung up. She sat down opposite me. 'Wouldn't it be a wonderful world if there were no more newspapers,' she said wistfully. 'No more lies. No more minor problems blown up into world disasters.'

'And nothing to light the fire with. But we might even save one or two rain-forests.'

Beth locked her eyes with mine. 'Now,' she said. 'Tell it all again . . . Oh, for God's sake! Who's this? You go.'

The lights of a car blazed across the kitchen curtains. We heard it pull up at the front of the house. A door slammed. When I opened the front door she already had her hand raised to press the bell. She was a well-built lady of slightly

144

more than my age and beginning to turn plump, well turned-out from her shiny pale hair to her fashionable yet country shoes. She was already speaking loudly in a high, nervous voice before her hand reached her side again – indeed, I had the unlikely impression that she had been speaking before I opened the door.

'Mr Cunningham? I hope you don't mind my coming without phoning first and I do hope that I haven't caught you at a bad time but I was on my way back from seeing the dentist in Dundee and it occurred to me that I was passing within a mile of here and when I spoke to my husband last night he asked me to come and see you.'

'Not at all,' I said feebly. It was too late to invite her inside. I had been backing down the hall away from her voice and her obtrusive femininity and she had pushed the door closed behind her and followed me.

'I'm Mrs Lansdyke – Helena Lansdyke nee Fordingbridge – and Arthur's still stuck in Switzerland so he phoned me last night and asked me to come and see Horace, although what I can tell him that you couldn't I don't know, and he knows that I'm not really into dogs anyway. But he said that he's made up his mind that he doesn't want Horace to linger if he's suffering and that if he isn't going to get better he'll have to be put down and he'll go along with whatever I decide.'

She paused. While I disentangled all the he's and made sense of what she had said, I was watching to see whether she drew a deep breath. There was no sign of it. Either she had trained as a singer or any movement of her ribs was lost behind a rather formidable bosom.

Her voice had fetched Beth out of the kitchen like a puppy on a check-lead. I tried to introduce her but Mrs Lansdyke was off again. 'It isn't a decision I'd want to make. I reminded Arthur that Horace and I have nothing in common but he said that he can't make the decision all the way from Switzerland and if he was going to have to start a new dog I should ask you to set one aside for him and make a start to the training. So I asked Duggie Henshaw—'

'He's still at home, is he?' Beth asked from behind Mrs Lansdyke's back.

'Oh, hello, my dear.' Mrs Lansdyke accepted Beth's presence without a blink. 'Yes, he'll be going back offshore in a day or two, always comes and goes on a Friday. I thought I'd get his opinion, because he does know about dogs and he's such a useful person to have about the place when he's there and not out shooting pigeons or doing odd jobs for people like Aubrey Stoneham. And he said that it's been ten days since Horace was shot, and none of us can think how that happened, but if he isn't walking again after ten days he probably never will. And if he does snare the occasional fox, good luck to him say I, coming round raking in the dustbins!'

I was dazed by the sudden flood of information, much of which seemed to be relevant when I could unscramble it. I decided that I could have saved myself a lot of trouble if I had sought out Mrs Lansdyke a week earlier.

'You'd better come and see him,' Beth said – meaning Horace, not Aubrey Stoneham, Dougal Henshaw or the fox. She led the way through the house and opened the door to the surgery.

Mrs Lansdyke swept inside and bent over Horace, who was still lying passively on his bed in the corner. He raised his head and looked at her without showing any sign of pleasure. 'So there you are, you lazy devil!' she said cheerfully. 'Serves you right for chasing off after the ladies or scrounging food from the neighbours. They must think we never feed you.' She put a hand down to pat Horace's head. He raised himself onto his forelegs and licked it. She turned away, wiped her hand on her skirt and then slapped a meaty thigh. 'Come on old chap. We're going home.' And she marched out of the surgery again while looking over her shoulder. Horace tried to rise, gave a feeble yelp and lay down again.

Beth closed the door.

'That settles it,' Mrs Lansdyke said. 'Put him down.'

'My partner, the vet, thinks that he's got into the habit of thinking of himself as crippled,' I said. 'She still hopes that he'll snap out of it.'

'If she wants him she can have him. Otherwise put him down.'

147

'We have a very good spayed bitch available,' Beth said. 'A field-trial winner on her second outing. And she's never wandered in her life, so you needn't worry about her going to visit the neighbours. Not that you'll have many neighbours left, soon.'

I had already wondered about disposing profitably of Lucy to a good home but had decided that any house where the man was often away and his wife disliked dogs could hardly be counted as 'good'. But Beth, it seemed, had introduced the subject in order to lead to another.

Mrs Lansdyke had arrived at the front door and prepared to open it for herself before I could get in front of her bulk. She stopped. 'They do seem to be melting away,' she said. 'I shan't miss that George Sievewright, smarming around the women and God alone knows how many of the babies in the district are his. Would you believe he even made a pass at *me*?'

Disbelief would have been appropriate but hardly flattering. Beth found a better formula. 'That seems just like the man,' she said.

'Doesn't it just? I'll miss Doris Ellingworth. We used to do our shopping together on Fridays and have lunch. But I must say I thought better of her than to go off without a word. There I was, the Friday before last, waiting in the hall with my hat on for her to come with her husband's car – Arthur had taken his to Glenrothes with him – and she never turned up. Of course, I thought that the woman who usually took Wanda – that's her youngest – had let her down, and it's no fun trailing around a supermarket with a child in tow. I couldn't get an answer on the phone so I thought that she must be taking Wanda to somebody else. It was the next day before I heard that she'd run off. Leaving her husband I can understand, the man's an idiot, and she could hardly take the children if she was going off with a lover, although I don't think it'll last, but she could at least have let me know that she wasn't coming, and nothing in the house for Arthur's dinner.

'How much are you asking for the bitch?' she continued, without any change of tone. When I told her (adding a margin as a deterrent) she pursed her lips as if for a kiss. I nearly stepped back. 'Outrageous!' she said. 'But it's his own money and if he wants to spend it on his dog instead of his wife that's up to him. I'll let him know. And now I must run, I'm going to dinner at the Stonehams and it'll take me an hour to get ready. Thank you so much for showing Horace to me. You know what to do.'

I took her to her car. She was still talking as she drove off but I couldn't hear a word. I went back to Beth.

'You know what that means?' Beth said.

'It means that we're stuck with Horace's keep from now on.' I knew that we would not put him down as long as there was the least hope of a recovery.

'That too,' Beth said. 'Now, come and sit down and tell it all to me again.'

I followed her into the kitchen and put on my most patient and hard-done-by expression, although in fact I was quite ready to go over it again. Saying it all aloud might give us the clue we so desperately needed. And, more, if Beth were to spot something, her questions might give me a hint which would save me from having to admit that my reasoning was a long way behind hers. A man has his pride.

We had progressed as far as my visit to the Old Manse when the phone rang. Beth grabbed it before I could get near it, but she had the grace to switch on the amplifier again.

It was Isobel's voice this time. 'We've just got home,' she said. 'You might like to know that Williamson's Land-Rover is tucked in behind the hedge at the bottom of the farm road. He always puts it there when he's heading for the pub and one of his real binges. If you want to catch him with his guard down, now's the best chance you're likely to get.'

Beth thanked her and disconnected. 'We may as well walk down,' she said. 'At least we can have a bar meal. My mind's too busy to think of cooking tonight.'

'I thought you wanted me to spill the rest of the story,' I said.

'You'll tell it better over a pint,' she said. 'Come on. We'll just look in on the new pups first and see that Sunspot has enough milk for them.'

We wrapped up against the cold, paid a respectful call on mother and pups in the whelping kennel, switched on the microphones and the radio link and set off on foot. Beth was quiet and I matched her silence. There could be ears in the darkness.

'What time does the moon come up?' she asked suddenly.

I thought about it. I usually have a mental picture of the phases of the moon, thanks to wild-fowling trips to the foreshore which are as regular as I can make them and Beth will allow. Adding on about forty minutes a day . . . 'Between midnight and one,' I said.

She only grunted.

We had reached the lights of the village street. In the hotel porch, she stopped. 'There's no reason now why we can't ask Mr Stoneham who gave him the photographs.'

'And he'll have no more reason to tell you than he had before. Somebody will have fed him a good story. In his mind, we're probably blackmailers or witches or something.'

She nodded. 'Leave it. We may have more leverage soon.'

The rambling bar of the old hotel was warm, cosily lit and nearly empty. Andrew Williamson was squatting malignantly on a stool at the bar. Beth would usually have gone to a table while I fetched drinks and a bar menu, but she followed me as I went to stand beside the farmer.

Florrie took my order. At the sound of my voice, Williamson looked round and focused on me. He was swaying slightly but otherwise seemed to be in control of his faculties. I tried to think of some inoffensive gambit to open a conversation.

He resolved my dilemma for me. 'Want to talk to you,' he said suddenly.

'Go ahead,' I told him.

'You can tell me something.'

I had been expecting abuse or complaint. In my relief I nearly asked whether he wanted anything specific, but I had the sense to hold my tongue.

'You ken my Brent?'

'Yes.' Brent was one of his working collie bitches, an evil-tempered animal but a clever worker. They had taken some prizes together at the sheepdog trials.

'The last day or two, she's not wanted to get out of her basket. Just wants to sleep. And drink.'

'She's not eating?' I asked.

'Not a damn thing.'

'How old is she?' I asked.

'Seven next May. What I want to know, could it be serious?'

Mid-life is a dangerous time for bitches. Remembering Lucy's pyometra I said, 'It could be very serious. And urgent. You'd better take her to a vet as soon as you can.'

Andrew Williamson was a tight man with his money but, to give him his due, he grudged his own dogs nothing. 'Yon mannie in the village won't have a surgery until the morn's afternoon. You think Mrs Kitts would take a look at her?'

'I should think so,' I said. 'I'll go and phone her.'

'Aye. Please,' he added. It was the first time that I ever heard him use the word. 'Tell her the wife's at home.'

The assumption that Isobel would be willing to brave the muddy and rutted farm track made sense. He was certainly in no condition to chauffeur dogs around the public roads. The reason for leaving his Land-Rover near the mouth of the farm road was that he could get home, across the fields if he could not follow the bend in the road, without leaving his own land. It was his belief that the breathalyser laws applied only on the public roads and he was probably correct.

'If Isobel decides that Brent needs to be spayed, that's all right?' I asked.

'Aye. Whatever she thinks. But' – he paused and blew his nose – 'if she thinks Brent needs putting down, tell her not to do it until I'm there. I want to be with her when she goes. She's been a good dog to me.'

153

'I don't think it'll come to that,' I said.

Florrie brought our drinks. I paid her, making sure that I had change for the telephone coin-box.

'Don't be a meanie,' Beth said. 'Aren't you going to offer Mr Williamson a drink?'

My relationship with the farmer had been such that blows rather than drinks were likely to be exchanged, but we seemed to be establishing a new rapport. 'Of course,' I said. 'What will you take?'

I added a large Glen Grant to my order, paid up and went off to the phone.

Isobel was none too pleased to be interrupted at her evening meal. 'I know all about needing to keep in with neighbouring farmers,' she said, 'and with Andrew Williamson in particular if he's at the root of this latest trouble. It may even take the pressure off us. But removing a pus-filled womb from a crabby and flea-ridden collie isn't my idea of an evening's relaxation when I've got other things on my mind.' I let her rattle on. I knew that the needs of the dog would be paramount in the end. 'I suppose I'll have to go,' she said at last. 'If it's pyometra, I'll take her back to the surgery. But I'll need a hand.'

'You'll get it,' I promised.

'Have you found out yet what's on Beth's mind?'

'I'm trying,' I said. 'I'm trying.'

Back at the bar, Williamson gave a grunt of

relief when I said that Isobel would be out to look at his collie within the hour. 'I'd not want anything to come over the old bitch for want of a wee bittie siller,' he said.

He had finished his whisky. Beth, who seemed to feel the need of a clear head, had settled for a half-pint of shandy and was holding the empty glass. The farmer looked at my beer-mug sitting full on the bar and ordered another whisky and a shandy for Beth. Florrie looked at him in mild surprise. He did not often put his hand in his pocket.

'Mr Williamson was telling me all about set-aside land, Beth said brightly. 'He thinks that it's an excellent idea.'

That did not surprise me. Any scheme that gave a farmer money for no work and at no risk from pests, the weather or falling prices would find favour in Williamson's eyes.

Beth gave me a meaning look. Evidently I was expected to carry the topic a stage further. I had no idea what she wanted but there seemed to be only one avenue open. 'George Sievewright agreed with you,' I said. 'But Dan seemed to be against it. Now that George is away, Dan's ploughing up the set-aside land. He says the ragwort got into it.'

'That can cost a braw penny,' Williamson said, nodding gravely. 'A terrible price, these selective wilkers. Weedkillers,' he corrected himself. He paid for his round of drinks, counting out the coins with care. 'A terrible price,' he repeated. 'But George was all for the set-aside scheme and he was senior partner.'

'George owned more than a half-share, did he?' Beth asked.

Williamson waved a contemptuous hand and nearly spilled his whisky. He drank it quickly before disaster could occur. 'George didn't own a damn thing,' he said. 'Nor Dan. Only the stock and machinery and the standing crops. It's rented. But George was the elder brother and that's the way their dad willed the tenancy. Not because George was the older, I'm thinking, but because George was a chip off the old block. Left a wheen of bastards around Fife and Tayside did old George Sievewright.'

'Who's the farm rented from?' Beth asked quickly.

'Yon land's a' part of Mr Stoneham's estate.'

I was taking a pull at my pint of stout and I nearly choked on it. Beth, who seemed less taken aback, gave me a warning headshake and a nudge. 'It's your round,' she said.

She had only taken half of her second shandy but I bought her another and renewed the farmer's whisky.

'I wonder how George is settling in on the west coast,' Beth said. 'Has anybody heard from him yet? Or is he too busy looking for a new lady-friend?'

The farmer gave vent to a short crack of laughter. 'Dod's no' on the west coast,' he said. 'That's just a tale they put about to save face. Run off wi' yon Mrs Ellingworth, so he has. Been carrying on for months, aabody kenned that except Ellingworth himself. Her Dada has a big spread in Wiltshire, the way I hear it, and can't thole his son-in-law. George reckons to fuck himself into a fortune. And the best of luck to him. She's a fine wee woman and there's a few years of childbearing left in her.'

Beth, it seemed, had ordered a steak for me and scampi for herself. They arrived on the bar and I dug into my pocket again to pay for them. She unwrapped her cutlery from its napkin but then put it down.

'I'll have to go now,' she said. 'Mr Williamson can eat my scampi. No,' she added to me. 'I can walk home on my own. You stay here and eat your steak. Then see if Isobel needs help with Mr Williamson's collie. Do you have the keys of the car on you?'

I gave her the keys. 'I thought there was some more you wanted me to tell you,' I said.

'There was, but I don't need it now.' She kissed me on the cheek. 'Don't wait up for me.'

She was gone, leaving three quarters of a pint of shandy on the bar, before I could ask her what the devil was going on.

'Yon's a grand quyne,' Williamson said. 'As well for you that George Sievewright's away south.' He chuckled evilly and then forgot my presence, attacking the scampi in his fingers and washing it down with shandy.

## TEN

I took out the pocket radio receiver. The dogs were quiet. If the equipment was in order, as it usually was, there were no intruders at home. I listened for a few moments and heard Horace move and whimper. All was well. I took my steak over to a table and ate most of it, slowly, while I tried to work out what Beth was up to.

Perhaps she was taking the opportunity to search Andrew Williamson's outbuildings for Stardust while the farmer was safely in the pub. But for that purpose she would hardly have taken my car. And it was far too late to do anything about the elopement of a farmer with a neighbour's wife, an event which might be romantic but was not unusual. My mind roamed onward. Dougal Henshaw now. If he had taken a couple of shots at Horace, perhaps for mauling the valuable pelt of the snared fox, he would certainly not want me spilling the beans to Arthur Lansdyke, his landlord, and putting the tenancy of his home at risk. But—

The radio relayed a short outburst of barks, not alarmed but rather an announcement that somebody had arrived. Isobel would be at Three Oaks. I thought that I heard the sound of a car.

A minute or two later her voice came over the radio. 'If anyone's listening, I've got Brent with me and I need some help.'

I left the rest of my steak and an inch or two of Guinness and hurried up the road.

Horace was still occupying the surgery but Walnut had been moved in with one of the brood bitches for company, leaving the isolation kennel free. While Isobel was leading Brent indoors, I carried Horace all the way and opened the full-sized door in the back of the kennel to put him down on the dog-bed. He sniffed suspiciously at his new accommodation but seemed to accept his demotion as no more than was to be expected in this rotten world. I gave him a pat and told him that it was a dog's life.

Brent might be a long way below par but she had no intention of allowing strangers to shove needles into her. I got a good grip on her collar and held tight while Isobel gave the anaesthetic. The collie bitch's reproductive system was in a mess. I passed instruments and held things while Isobel operated. It was past midnight before we had finished and cleaned up but there was no sign of Beth. I gave Isobel a small drink and packed her off home.

For a while I dawdled, expecting Beth to return or phone at any moment, but soon I gave her up and went to bed. I meant to lie awake and wait for her, but suddenly there was daylight and morning had arrived. This was the day on which we would sink or swim among the sharks of the press and the bed beside me was cold and undisturbed. I thought that I remembered the sound of a car in the night or the very early morning, but it might have been a dream.

Fumbling in haste, I dressed and went down to the kitchen. From the surgery I could hear a furious growling. The makings of my breakfast were neatly set out on the table. Beside them was a note.

> *You were sleeping like a baby so I didn't want to wake you yet. Pups have been fed. Back soon.*

It seemed that Beth had been neither murdered nor kidnapped during the night. I got on with breakfast. While I was picking my way through some cereal Isobel arrived, looking played out.

'You're early,' I said. 'After last night's triumph of modern surgery, I thought you'd sleep in.'

'With reporters coming this morning? You must be joking. After about three hours' sleep I woke up at five, convinced that the entire media, complete with television cameras, were about to arrive and find me in my nightdress. How's the patient?'

'Sounds hung over. I didn't dare to go in.'

'I'll phone Williamson to come and collect her later.' Isobel's lip had curled in a sneer at my pusillanimity, but I noticed that she was no keener than I was to face a notoriously fractious collie just out of the anaesthetic and upset by the strangeness of her surroundings. 'Where's Beth?' she asked.

'Damned if I know. She was out most of the night. She left a note but it doesn't help much. Ask her yourself,' I added. The car that was arriving at the door had the clattering valves and rattling exhaust peculiar to my old estate car.

Beth plunged into the house like a spaniel following a scent into cover. She was wearing Wellingtons and one of my waxproofed coats, all liberally muddied, but otherwise she was dressed as she had been in the pub. 'Sorry I'm late,' she said breathlessly. 'Had to wait and make sure that they'd followed their usual Thursday routine.'

'Who or what—?' I began.

She ignored my attempt at a question while shedding the coat and boots into a corner. 'John, will you put Horace in the car, please? Have you eaten a good breakfast?'

'You mean Walnut?'

'Don't mess about, I mean Horace. I may want to see if he reacts to places.'

'Beth!' Isobel said loudly. Beth stopped and looked at her, puzzled. 'Beth, will you sit down for a moment and tell us what's going on.'

Beth wound up again. 'No time for that. I've already phoned round the large contractors fro the call-box outside that pub at the crossroads. I struck lucky. One of them can send off half a dozen labourers in a van straight away. We've got to get moving.' She sat down to lace her brogues. 'Isobel, can you phone Henry to come and keep things ticking over?'

'I suppose so,' Isobel said. In addition to being played out, she was now looking slightly stunned.

'Tell him to bring his car. Then, when the reporter and photographer arrive . . .' Beth paused for a split second's thought. 'If they're too early, say in the next hour and a half, keep them talking. Tell them the story, show them the photograph – it's on the table next door – and take them to look at the oak tree. Let them meet Walnut. Spin it out a bit. Then bring them to the Old Manse. Will you do that?'

'I—'

'And get hold of the local Bobby and bring him along.'

'He's off today. I saw him drive off in civvies as I walked by,' Isobel said. She seemed relieved to have something factual to say.

'Then the call will be relayed to Cupar,' Beth said. 'Try to get hold of John's friend, Constable . . .?' She looked at me.

'Peel,' I said.

'Constable Peel. Tell him that it's very important and urgent. Will you do all that?'

'I suppose so,' Isobel said. She ran her fingers

162

through her usually tidy hair. 'But – for God's sake, Beth – you'll have to tell me—'

'No time for that. We've got to be there before the men. John, is Horace in the car?'

'I'll go and get him,' I said.

'Put a warm coat on.'

I put a warm coat on and went out. I carried Horace back from the isolation kennel to the car, where Beth had already opened the rear door for me and installed herself in the driver's seat. Horace stirred uneasily in my arms at this evidence that he was to travel again. The car had been through a carwash only a few days earlier but it looked as though it had taken part in an autocross in the rain.

Beth was wolfing a hastily buttered roll. As soon as I was more or less in the passenger's seat she pushed the second half of it into her mouth and let the clutch out. The car set off with a jerk, clattering gravel against its own underside.

We went through the village like a greyhound coursing a hare. When we passed the derestriction sign, she speeded up. Her mouth was almost too full for her to chew the remains of her roll, let alone to answer questions, and I wanted all her concentration to be on the road. The Old Manse was almost in sight before she managed to empty her mouth.

'Why the hurry?' I asked.

Beth wiped her mouth with her sleeve. 'We have to be there before the men,' she said. 'I told you. And we have to look as though we belong there. I don't want the car still pinging and clicking.'

'It'll ping and click for an hour if you don't slow down,' I said. She covered the last quarter-mile at a more sedate pace, pulled into Tony Ellingworth's yard and parked against the gable. The place seemed to be deserted but his van was tucked in behind the house, half hidden.

Beth saw me looking at it. 'Dan Sievewright picked him up,' she said. 'They took the youngest child with them – to drop off with Mr Buccleugh's daughter, I suppose. The older ones went off to school. I had to bank on them doing what they always do on Thursdays. They wouldn't want to start people talking. Let's take a look at Horace.'

I opened the rear door. Horace took one look around, sniffed the air and curled up into a shivering ball. I gave him a pat and closed the door. Without raising his head, he looked up at me through the glass with apprehensive eyes.

'That's what I wanted to be sure about,' Beth said. 'Come on. We'd better stand at the front door as though we'd just come out of it.' But when we reached the Ellingworth doorstep, she looked at me doubtfully. 'There may be a lot of standing around,' she said. 'Are you sure you're warm enough? You could go for a drive or something.'

I was wearing a coat which was almost too warm for the mild day. 'The cold doesn't bother me,' I said. 'What does worry hell out of me is that you're taking the law into your own hands and you haven't given me the least hint that you know what you're doing. You could land us with a lawsuit, if nothing worse. Shouldn't you have told the police instead of rushing in?'

Beth smothered a yawn. She was looking very tired. Now that she had no urgent action to buoy her up she seemed ready to doze on her feet, but her mind was working away, somewhere beyond the fog of exhaustion. 'If we call the police,' she said sleepily, 'they won't take action until long after you've been pilloried in the press. Do you want to go through the rest of your life being addressed as "Shock Horror" by any rival competitor who wants to unsettle you? Imagine a two-page spread of those photographs, with your face somewhere near the top and quotes from a whole lot of self-styled experts. They could retract for ever afterwards, but we'd still be out of business. It's worth a bit of risk, isn't it?'

'How much of a risk?'

'I don't know. You'd better speak to the men when they come. They'll take orders better from a man.'

I was quite used to having this particular buck passed to me although it was not Beth's gender but her apparent youth that diminished her authority.

'We're Mr and Mrs Ellingworth,' she said more briskly. 'We live here. Our water supply's gone off and we think there's a break over there, where the bonfire was.' She pointed towards the scar, a disc of white ash with a fringe of blackened material. 'It's urgent, because of the children. Lay it on thick.'

'What if they don't find anything?' I asked.

She giggled nervously. 'Then I should think we run for it,' she said.

There was no time for more questions. A Transit van pulled in from the road and five men piled out. The driver, a cocky little man with bright eyes, was also the foreman. I repeated Beth's words to him, almost verbatim.

'Plastic pipe?' he asked.

It seemed easiest to agree.

'What were you thinking of, lighting a fire above it? Well, we'd better see what damage you've done.'

He called the men over and they started to dig. Beth nudged me and led the way towards the hedge as if we were inspecting our garden. I was beginning to see how her mind was working. Not that the working of her mind was important. What mattered was that she had to be right first time. 'Why there, for God's sake?' I asked her.

'Where do you think I've been for half the night?' she countered peevishly. As if the mention had reminded her, she put her whole being into an enormous yawn. 'This is the only place.'

'There's a whole farm just beyond the hedge.

You can't have scoured the whole place for turned earth?'

'Not all of it. The fields overlooked from where Mr Buccleugh lives didn't seem very likely. And a lot of it's taken up with stubble and winter barley. Any digging there would have shown up, even by moonlight.'

'But the set-aside land.' I looked through the hedge to where the fresh ploughing showed in a great rectangle of raw red earth.

'That was the first place I looked at. You said that only the first strip had been ploughed before Horace was shot. The rest was done much later, after Mr Sievewright's tractor part came. I looked at the first bit very carefully. It had been ploughed before that heavy thunderstorm, because the earth had been beaten down by rain. The crumb structure – what do you call it, tilth? – was destroyed over the first five or six furrows. The surface was almost polished. And I thought, what better way to cover up freshly dug earth than to light a bonfire above it? And the scent. Especially the scent.'

She was losing me again. 'What about the new rose bushes along at the farmhouse?' I asked.

'I looked there. They were planted ages ago. I was going to dig here but I didn't dare. Dark earth among the white ash, almost opposite the front door, would have stood out like I don't know what.'

That put another ten questions into my mind,

but we were interrupted. 'You'd better come and see this,' the foreman called. He stooped and took a look for himself. 'It's a dead dog.'

'You go,' Beth said hoarsely. 'I don't think I could bear to look, in case I've got it all wrong.'

I walked over to the excavation, hoping that I had read Beth's mind correctly. The remains were unpleasant but still quite well preserved. They had been a collie, not a springer spaniel. 'My brother's dog,' I said. 'I didn't know that he'd buried her here. Move her aside and go on digging.'

'Any deeper and the heat wouldn't've reached the pipe,' the foreman said. 'And there's no sign of leaking water.'

'You're not down to unbroken clay, are you?' I asked. I held my breath.

He heeled a spade into the ground. 'No. This has been dug.'

I breathed again. 'Go on down a bit further,' I said.

Beth had circled past towards the entrance drive. I joined her. 'It's all right,' I said. 'It's not Stardust. It's a collie.'

She nodded. 'George Sievewright's collie bitch. They'd have to get rid of her too. That's what Horace was digging for, the smell of a bitch in season. And, as I said, the bonfire wouldn't only cover up the dug earth, it would kill the scent. Dan Sievewright couldn't admit that Horace had been after his brother's collie, so he told you that Mr Ellingworth's spaniel was on heat.'

'But . . . but how could you be so sure?' I asked her. 'I was homing in on Dougal Henshaw. He does odd jobs for Aubrey Stoneham and he wouldn't want to get in Arthur Lansdyke's bad books and be kicked out of his cottage.'

She shook her head. In her tired state, the movement almost made her lose her balance. I caught her elbow. 'He wasn't here,' she said. 'Work it out for yourself. He goes offshore, two weeks on and two off, coming and going on Fridays. The day he arrived home, Mrs Ellingworth failed to turn up to meet Mrs Lansdyke.

'There isn't any single thing, as in the plays on the telly. It just all adds up, if you look at it the right way round. What could be so damning that somebody went to all that trouble to stop you asking questions? Well, think about it. What questions were you asking?'

'About Horace,' I said.

'Right. So why was Horace important? Because,' Beth said, answering several of her own questions, 'Horace had been shot to stop him digging. If you asked enough questions, you might have found out why and where.

'Next, when would George Sievewright be carrying on with Mrs Ellingworth?'

That was another easy question. 'All the damn time, from what we've been hearing,' I said.

'Rubbish! While he's working a farm with his

169

brother, and while her husband's around the smallholding?' Beth dredged up a grin from somewhere. 'Obviously you've got no experience of carrying on, I'm glad to see. Thursdays, you ass, when his brother and her husband went off to the market at Dunfermline together and always stopped off at the Cardenden Gun Club on the way home. But that Thursday, two weeks ago, there was a thunderstorm moving up from the south-west. It would have broken over Dunfermline and the Cardenden Club ages before it reached here. They wouldn't stay and shoot clay pigeons in the pouring rain. So Mr Ellingworth would have arrived home unexpectedly. If you want a clincher, there were signs that cloth had been burned on the bonfire. Clothes, perhaps. Or bedsheets.'

'You'll get hell from the police for spoiling the evidence,' I said. 'Or rather, I will.'

Beth raised a hand to brush away that little problem as insignificant. 'The evidence is still there. We've just rearranged it a little. Put what I've said together with all sorts of other things. Why did Dan Sievewright tell you not to shoot over his land any more and then change his mind when you told him that Horace wouldn't be fit to go shooting for months if ever?'

'Dan Sievewright's involved?'

'Well, of course he is. George would never have let Dan plough up the set-aside land. So why was Dan already ploughing it when, from what he'd said to you, George was only away looking at another farm? How did he know that George wasn't coming back? The brothers never got on. And the farm's only rented. It was Dan's chance to get the farm to himself, plus a few fields that he owned instead of renting and a smaller, comfortable house instead of that big tumbledown barrack of a place. I'll bet he drove the bargain of a lifetime with Mr Ellingworth.'

'Blackmail?'

'They call it negotiating from strength,' Beth said.

I was still struggling to fit the pieces of the puzzle together when a large and dirty car, comparatively new but already bearing the signs of much hard use, pulled in behind the van. Isobel was in the front passenger's seat. She put up both hands in a gesture of helplessness.

'They're miles too early,' Beth said indignantly. 'But we can use up some time. I hope it's enough. There's something I haven't told you.'

'There's a hell of a lot you haven't told me,' I retorted, but she had already turned away towards the contractor's van.

The man who bobbed up out of the driver's seat of the car was obviously a reporter – young, hyperactive and brash. He was dark, with a predatory face. His clothes were scruffy, but his scruffiness was a different brand from Tony Ellingworth's, being the kind of big-city scruffiness that is a calculated gesture in the face of the establishment and which pays good money to have its leather jacket stained and its jeans vandalised by a competent designer before deigning to wear them. An older man, carrying an expensive camera, climbed more slowly out of the back.

We were well within earshot of the labourers and the reporter was about to utter my name. My mind stalled but Beth, who must have been close to exhaustion, still had her wits about her. 'Here you are at last,' she said. 'Come with me. I've something to show you.' She led the way past the house towards the outbuildings that fringed a small barn. She was carrying a short crowbar. The back of the contractor's van was standing open and I guessed that she had abstracted it from there.

As I moved after them, wondering what tricks Beth could still pull, Isobel caught up with me. 'I'm sorry,' she whispered. 'I couldn't hold them any longer. Is it a disaster?'

'Probably,' I said.

Beth took us to a shed which was as ramshackle as the rest of the buildings. She stopped and caught my eye. 'This is what I was doing for the other half of the night – driving around and using the silent whistle. I didn't know which houses Walnut's real owner and his friend lived in, so I woke up every dog in the village. At the two farms, I just set collies barking. This is the only place I got a response that sounded like the right

172

one and I had to get out in a hurry because lights were coming on. You know how Stardust yips when she hears one of us coming, whistling.' She caught the reporter's eye. 'Mrs Kitts showed you the other spaniel?'

'She did.' The reporter looked stern. 'It was obviously scared out of its wits.'

'By you?'

The reporter could recognise a loaded question when a victim dared to point one at him. He changed ground quickly. 'Mrs Kitts said that it was a ringer.'

'It is. Now take a look here.' The shed's door was divided like a stable door. The upper half was secured by a new-looking hasp and padlock. She pushed the crowbar into the widest gap. 'I think that our dog is in here.'

I knew that she was right. At the sound of our voices a dog inside the shed set up a hullabaloo. A dog's voice is often more distinctive than its appearance and I recognised Stardust. I felt a flood of relief, more for Stardust herself than for my reputation.

The upper half of the door splintered and swung open under Beth's attack. There was no need to open the lower half. Stardust treated it as a fence and came over in a huge leap. She raced round us in a mad circle and then took another leap, straight up into my arms, and began to lick my face. I could hear the camera clicking and whirring.

'Do you see the resemblance?' Beth asked. Stardust leaped out of my arms to jump up against her and then came back to me.

In spite of himself, the reporter was impressed. He produced a small tape recorder. 'So what's it all about?' he asked.

We had begun to walk back towards the cars. Beth stopped. I could see that she was playing for time. 'A gentleman who lives further along this road brought us his dog. That's the spaniel in the back of our car. Somebody had shot at him and tried to kill him. That was almost a fortnight ago, but he still can't get up onto his feet. There'd been no reports of sheep-worrying for weeks. This bothered us. We have a stock of dogs and pups and they aren't always tight to heel. So John – Captain Cunningham—'

'Mister,' I said.

'So Mr Cunningham asked a few questions. Somebody thought that he might find out too much about something much more serious and decided to get a weapon to hold over us. And, when that didn't work, they wanted to put us out of business altogether. They knew where there was a spaniel that had been ill-treated and which they could fake to look like Stardust here. And they had one genuine photograph of Mr Cunningham. Show them, John. Do what you do when a dog's getting over-excited.'

Stardust was circling round me. I told her to sit, but in her relief at being back among friends

174

she only wanted to dance. I stooped and lifted my hand. She sat quickly, grinning idiotically. She knew perfectly well that I would not have smacked her for anything short of stealing our Sunday dinner. The absence of any real fear was obvious even to one who knew nothing of dogs.

The reporter was leafing through a handful of prints similar to those that Aubrey Stoneham had shown us. 'I see what you're suggesting,' he said. 'But have you any proof?'

'We're giving it to you as fast as we can,' Beth said. We had moved on as far as the corner of the house. I saw her glance in the direction of the workmen. They were working steadily and the pile of displaced earth was beginning to loom over them.

We seemed to have finished with Stardust for the moment. I walked her at heel to the car and put her in with Horace.

'We called in Mr Hautry of the SSPCA,' Beth was saying when I returned to the group. 'He thinks that they altered the markings of the dog you saw, using black dye, to increase her resemblance to this one. He took some hair samples for testing. You'll get the results as soon as we know them.'

The reporter thought it over and nodded slowly. 'We could hold off long enough for that,' he said. 'But you'll have to answer one more question. Without the answer, the whole thing makes no sense. What was the "something more serious" they were so uptight about?'

Beth cast another agonised glance at the workmen who were still steadily digging. They might think that we were in the wrong place, but as long as we were ready to pay they were willing to dig. She made another play for time. 'Look,' she said, 'are you going to let me tell this in my own way or do I give the story to some other rag and leave you to read about somebody else's scoop?'

I saw his disbelief rekindle. 'Go on, then,' he said. 'Tell it your own way.'

Beth paused for thought. From this point on, it seemed to me that we had no more than speculation to offer. To help her out, I embarked on a rambling explanation, beginning with the thunderstorm and hoping against hope that I would be interrupted before I had to make any slanderous allegations which I would not be able to prove and which might even turn out to be wrong.

The interruption arrived in good time but it was not the one for which I was hoping. A Mercedes of the current registration pulled in behind the reporter's car and was forced to stop there. Dan Sievewright was in the driver's seat. Out of the other door erupted a furious Tony Ellingworth, gobbling like a turkey. As much of his face as was visible was scarlet and even his beard seemed to have flushed with fury.

'What the hell's going on here?' he demanded. And then, when he saw the workmen at their digging, he tried to rush forward. 'Stop!' he screamed. 'Stop!'

I stepped forward and caught his coat, bringing him to a halt. Such was his fury that everybody else seemed to take a step back. He turned and swung a punch at me but he was an unskilled fighter and I had once been a highly trained soldier. I ducked under his fist, swung him round and held him by the elbows – at arms' length, to avoid the heels that he aimed at my shins and any risk to my genitals from his fists. He was still shouting. He struggled to face me but I held on.

We had not heard the arrival of yet another car but our grim dance was interrupted when a voice with a faintly Irish accent said, 'What's the problem here? Calm down now, everybody, and tell me what this is about.'

The voice was backed by a dark uniform. Silence fell, the calm before the storm. Constable Peel had arrived rather in advance of his cue.

I let Ellingworth jerk out of my grip. He faced the constable. 'These men are digging on my land and without my permission. Get them out of here. Now.'

Peel met my eye. 'Is this true?' he asked.

I hesitated.

The foreman had left his work and joined us. 'That's what I want to know,' he said. 'This gentleman' – pointing at me – 'led me to believe that he was the occupier. He has us digging for a water-pipe that I don't believe's there. And what I want to know is, who's going to pay for a' this work.'

'You'll be paid,' I said. I could feel my face prickling with embarrassment.

'No you bloody well won't,' Ellingworth said furiously. 'Not by me. Pack up your tools and get off my land right away. And as for you,' he turned on me, 'I'm going to prosecute.'

'For digging your garden?' I asked him. 'There's no law of trespass in Scotland.'

Ellingworth's answer would have interested me but he was never to make it. The labourers had continued their work. Arguments between employers were of no concern to them. They had been told to dig, so they dug. There was a sudden shout.

'Maybe they've found a water-pipe after all,' the foreman said.

One of the men came running towards us. 'There's a hand,' he said shakily. 'Poking up out of the earth. I thought it was a root and I bent to pull it up. There's a body in there.' The other workmen were standing beside the hole, staring.

'I think you'll find,' Beth said, 'that there are two.'

Ellingworth cast a desperate look around but the entrance was obstructed by the constable's car and escape on foot over the fields was out of the question. He had gone from red to white.

'These people seem to know more about it than I do,' he said hoarsely. 'I think you'll agree that they have some questions to answer.'

Peel was already speaking into the personal radio that was clipped to his breast pocket, identifying himself to his controller. 'I'm at the Old Manse at Colm,' he said. 'Please tell Inspector McLean that I have a report of a dead body. Am investigating. Out. And now,' he said, 'you will all stand back and disturb nothing. Come away from there,' he told the workmen.

We gathered into a large group. I found Dan Sievewright standing beside me. 'We thought you'd gone to Dunfermline,' I said.

He shook his head. He seemed both amused and detached. 'There was a roup at one of the farms near Pitscottie. No' a damn thing worth bidding for in the sale, so we're back early.' He managed to attract Constable Peel's attention. 'This is nothing to do wi' me,' he said. 'If you'll move your car, I'll awa' hame.'

'If it was nothing to do with you,' Beth said into a sudden hush, 'why were you telling everybody your brother had moved to a farm on the west coast when he's buried here with his dog and Mrs Ellingworth?'

The reporter was putting a fresh cassette into his recorder and I saw the photographer hurriedly changing his film.

Dan Sievewright was looking murder at Beth but he had found his voice again. 'I honest-to-

God thought they'd run off together,' he said. 'But I wasn't about to tell the whole world that. This is the first I knew of them being buried. If it's them,' he added hastily.

Ellingworth must have known that it was too late for bluff. At this attempt to leave him to face the music alone, he lost his head completely. 'That bugger!' he shouted. 'He helped me bury them.' A silence fell, so complete that I could hear the call of a distant pigeon and the whirr of the reporter's tape.

Ellingworth's position was hopeless. After his outburst, he gave up all attempt at evasion. 'We were rained off,' he said, 'and I got home early. I found them together. I heard their voices upstairs as soon as I got in the door. There was a cast-iron doorstep that came from my mother's house. I took it with me—'

PC Peel had his pocket book in his hand but I saw him glance at the tape-recorder and give up any attempt at verbatim notes. He dropped the book back into his pocket and groped for handcuffs. 'I must warn you,' he said hastily, 'that—'

Ellingworth was in no mood to heed the customary warning. What began as a confession had become a plea for sympathy. His voice rose above the constable's. 'We had to bury them before it was time for the kids to come home. I told them their mother had gone away . . .'

Even in my relief, I found the scene distressing. The details were no concern of mine. I turned away and Beth walked with me. 'We'd better stick around,' she said. 'There'll be arrangements to make about the children. Perhaps Mr Buccleugh's daughter will look after them for the moment. I think Mrs Ellingworth had a sister in Edinburgh.'

'That should give Charles Buccleugh a fresh interest in life,' I said weakly.

'As soon as we're free to go, I want the car. The reporters will give you a lift home. They'll need your story.'

'Where are you going?' I asked.

'I want to pay a call on Aubrey Stoneham,' she said. There was a smile of anticipation on her tired face. 'I think I've earned the right to tell him what I think of him and what publicity's coming his way. And there's one other thing we could get out of this,' she said.

'What's that?'

'I don't suppose that Mr Randall knew why they wanted the fake photographs. They'll have spun him a tale. If we can get to him while he's feeling guilty and trying to prove that he didn't know anything about any murders—'

'He'll exonerate me,' I said.

Beth waved that away as irrelevant. 'We may be able to get Walnut's pedigree off him,' she said. 'We could well argue that he's already made us a present of her.'

'More negotiation from strength?' I suggested.

She smiled and shook her dark curls. 'Just

plain old-fashioned blackmail. If the pedigree looks good . . . we'll need at least one more brood bitch if Stardust won't stand—'

She broke off. We had arrived back at the car and, out of long habit, stooped to look in and see that the dogs were all right.

They were more than all right. Horace had forgotten about being an invalid. He was on his feet. He was also on Stardust. He was firmly mounted and working away like any other sex maniac. Stardust was standing for him. As is normal (with bitches as with ladies, when caught in the act) she looked ashamed and yet distinctly pleased with herself.

Beth sighed. 'I can never get over the feeling that it's really quite romantic,' she said. 'It's silly, but there it is. Other people get soppy over weddings so I don't see why I shouldn't feel sentimental when dogs fall in love. Tell me, what made you choose the name Walnut?'

'It just came to me,' I said.

We very much hope you have enjoyed
this Large Print Book

If you would like to find out about
our range of other titles,
you can either enquire at your
local library or contact
the publishers by writing to us at:

Remploy Press
Lightowler Road
Hanson Lane
Halifax
HX1 5NB
or by telephone on 0422 350517

Our policy at Remploy Press is to
continually improve our product and
we would welcome any suggestion or
ideas of additional titles you may
have, from you . . . our valued readers